I0685827

BLOOD AVENGED

SONS OF NAVARUS
BOOK 1

K.M. SCOTT

WRITING AS
GABRIELLE BISSET

Published in the United States

ISBN 13: 978-1-955335-35-5

BLOOD AVENGED

I am everything you desire. I am vampire.

Powerful and manipulative, Vasilije does as he pleases. A vampire beholden to no one, he takes what he desires, drinking deeply the pleasures this life has to offer.

WHEN ONE OF his own is staked, Vasilije must travel to New Orleans to exact his revenge. There he meets Sasa, a beautiful woman who arouses him like no other has for centuries. Vasilije's need for vengeance is equaled only by his passion for her, but what he finds in his revenge is just the beginning...

1

I am everything you desire.
I am everything you fear.
I am lust and appetite.
I am vampire.

The beat of the music slammed into his body like crushing blows from an angry attacker, each note reverberating in his bones. He sat perfectly still and let the beat thrum through him as he picked up the seductive scent wafting across the crowded room, carried by a thick cloud of cigarette smoke. Undetected by all but him, its subtle sweetness teased his nose with a promise of what was to come.

Scanning the room, he watched like a bird tracking its prey. All of humanity seemed to file past him. Desperate, drunk, and powerless, the crowd was a smorgasbord laid out especially for him. With no effort at all, he could have any of them. The brunette dancing between two men, her movements telegraphing that her sex was needy for what they offered. If he chose, in seconds, they'd be gone and she'd be his for the taking. The tanned, muscular male eyeing him from three tables away, who he sensed preferred what hung between his legs to what the brunette offered. The barely legal blonde, whose wide green eyes betrayed just how much of life she hadn't experienced despite the lies her body told.

He could have any of them.

Vasilije watched his victim at the bar. Every bat of an eyelash he felt. Every clank of the ice against the glass he heard as if he were there himself. The distance between them meant nothing.

Through the tightly packed crowd, he saw the woman next to his target lean over, obscuring his view. He watched as she pressed her body next to the man's, a not-so-subtle hint to her interest.

The sweet scent remained, and Vasilije closed his eyes to enjoy it, not interested in the woman or her pathetic attempt to seduce his prey away.

He had no idea the vampire waited patiently for his moment. Vasilije liked the idea that ignorance was bliss. For now. In a few short minutes, another bliss would take them both over, and he'd have what he'd eyed for days.

The man made a move toward the door and every cell in Vasilije's body came alive. Two steps and he was in the thick of the crowd, their bodies pressing up against his as he brushed by them. He weaved through the group like a dark secret whispered from one person to another.

At the exit, he inhaled deeply, his sense of smell filtering out the putrid mixture of exhaust, perfume, and stale alcohol that hovered at the entrance to the street. Only his prey's scent remained, imprinted on him.

He was nearby.

Closing his eyes, Vasilije let his other senses take over. The sound of the man's shoes hitting the pavement echoed in his ears. The feel of his prey's blood pumping through his body throbbed against Vasilije's cool skin, matching his heartbeat.

So healthy. So alive.

He'd tracked him for days, his desire growing with each passing moment. It had taken little time for him to decide he would make him one of his kind. He stirred something inside that hadn't been touched for years.

Such a soul would be a perfect addition to his world.

He moved away from the noise of the club into the streets of London as he gained ground on his target. Now in his view, the man moved much faster. Did he sense the danger that lurked nearby? But it was no use. He would surrender this night.

Vasilije walked calmly, never losing sight of the man. He sensed his fear and took it into himself, relishing the sensation. How long had it been since he'd felt fear—true fear that stole one's breath away and paralyzed the limbs?

A quick left onto a darkened street and his prey broke into a full run, his fear morphing into pure terror that surged through Vasilije's veins. In his ears, he heard the man's heart pound faster and faster, his body reacting to his mind's screams.

Into the night air, he whispered, "Come to me," and waited for the man to make his way back to him. With each step, Vasilije moved closer, but the man remained out of reach.

Something or someone was helping him escape.

Quickly, Vasilije scanned the area, his eyes darting left and right in the darkness. Was there another of his kind close? He sensed no one, but someone was interrupting his pursuit.

Reluctantly, he accepted the situation and disappeared into thin air, reappearing just mere feet in front of the man. Stunned, he skidded to a stop against Vasilije's chest.

"No more running."

His hand moved to the man's chin and gently held him. Eyes filled with a fear he'd seen a thousand times before stared back at him, pleading for mercy from a being that possessed none.

His voice a deep timbre now, Vasilije began to hypnotize the man. "I've waited long enough for you."

To his surprise, the trick didn't work. The man's eyes grew wide, and he opened his mouth to speak, but only weak cries came out. Why was he able to resist?

"Who are you?"

"Alex," he said, his voice almost a whimper.

"Alex, I want you to look into my eyes. Listen to my voice."

"Please don't kill me."

Vasilije stroked the man's cheek and leaned in next to his ear. "I'm going to give you a life you've never dreamed of, Alex."

"Please! Take all my money. Just let me go. I have a girlfriend. Tatiana. I don't want to die!"

Vasilije thought back to the only Tatiana he'd ever known in his over four-hundred-year existence. Grimacing, he returned his focus to Alex's eyes and pushed his memory of the past out of his mind.

"Well, maybe I'll let you have her."

"Please don't do this!" the man begged, his blue eyes filling with tears.

Cradling his face in his hands, Vasilije concentrated on Alex, and slowly whatever had been protecting him slipped away. His lids became heavy, obscuring his eyes, and the fear left his mind and body.

"Alex." Vasilije let the name rest on his tongue as he hissed out the last syllable. "Mine."

The muscles in Alex's body gave in to his power and all fight evaporated from him. He slumped against the vampire's body as his mind finally succumbed to his persuasion.

Vasilije guided him to a building just a few steps away and leaned him against a stone wall. For a moment, he stilled to look at this human who had so captivated him, more than any other creature in years. His shoulder length blond hair shone like it had been touched each day by the sun. Vasilije gingerly touched the ends with his fingertips, feeling the sun's long forgotten warmth against his fingers.

His eyes moved over Alex's face, past his mouth and cheekbones to eyes hooded by slack lids. Within those slits were blue eyes that stared out passively at him. Eyes that saw what Vasilije commanded as he silently inserted ideas into the man's mind.

Nothing about Alex was unique individually, and despite admiring his beauty, Vasilije couldn't say that was what had drawn him to the human. It was something else, something about him that created the impression of the forbidden.

But now he would be his.

Vasilije's fangs slid seductively into his mouth as he eyed the gentle throbbing in Alex's neck. In just a few moments, they would sink into his skin and sweet blood would fill him. The thought of it made his mouth water.

Unlike the rest of his fellow vampires, he wasn't forced to live under the restrictions of vampire law and obtain permission to turn a human. His sire had been taken from the Earth years ago, and without her, he was free to sire anyone he pleased.

He was truly a being beholden to no one.

Alex would join the hundreds of others scattered across the globe who counted him as their sire. Inside, he knew where each one was at any given moment, like a piece of himself inside another. When he desired to have them around, they were. And when he preferred a life of solitude, the choice of many vampires, he sent them away.

But they were never truly gone.

He would keep Alex with him until he'd completed his initiation period. To do any less would be cruel. A newly turned vampire needed his sire for virtually every-thing to survive. His blood would nourish him, like no other's could. A human might give him what he needed for a short time, but it could never be what his sire's was. And his knowledge would help Alex learn how to be a vampire and how to grow accustomed to the new life he'd given him.

Vasilije softly pressed his mouth to his neck, feeling the warmth of his skin against his lips. Alex turned his head in response, and Vasilije lifted his head. Staring deeply into his eyes, he silently instructed him to turn his head.

His mouth returned to Alex's neck. As he watched the rhythmic pulse just under his skin, he slid his tongue over his fangs, enjoying the feel of their sharp points.

"Alex, from this moment on, I'm your sire. You belong to me."

Without moving his head, Alex moaned his unneeded agreement. For a long moment, the world around them stood still, as Vasilije pressed his fangs slowly into the tender skin. His canines pierced a vein and blood began to flood over his tongue. Its thickness oozed back toward his throat, the tangy taste sliding over his taste buds, exciting them.

How wonderful he tasted! As Alex's life flowed down Vasilije's throat, he fastened his mouth on his neck and pulled at the vein, careful to take only as much as he should. He'd bring Alex to the point of no return and then, as he lingered between life and death, he'd give him the first of many gifts a sire could provide.

Still human for the moment, Alex struggled against Vasilije's hold, but it was no use. A vampire for centuries, he had the strength of a bull and reflexes of a wild cat. At the first sign of resistance, he tightened his hold on the man's jaw and flung his leg over him, trapping his body between the wall and his own.

"It's futile to struggle," Vasilije whispered low in his ear. "Let it take you."

"Please..." Alex's voice faded to a groan as Vasilije's mouth tugged at his vein with more vigor.

"I want nothing else," Vasilije chuckled as he closed the holes he'd made in Alex's neck.

He carefully laid him on the ground, and as Alex fought to hold on to the last shred of his human life, Vasilije wiped the corners of his mouth. Licking the blood from his fingertips, he savored the taste as he knelt down beside the man who was to be his newest vampire.

Vasilije stroked the blond hair that would never again be touched by the warmth or light of the sun. His fingers glided over the sun kissed skin on Alex's face, which in moments would be reduced to a pallor common to those of the night. Even now, the warmth that had been present in his skin was gone.

Lifting his wrist to his mouth, Vasilije sunk his fangs into his skin to open a vein. Blood ran freely in a stream from his wrist, and he pulled Alex to him to begin the transition from human to vampire. Near death, his head had to be held to Vasilije's wrist, but as if it were his true nature, Alex began drinking seconds after tasting his sire's blood, eagerly sucking the liquid into his mouth.

For Vasilije, this was the part he enjoyed. To feed from the neck of a human could sustain him for a short time, but to take from another like him and give in return was a far more satisfying experience.

Alex's mouth sucked greedily at his wrist, drinking his sire's blood as readily as he'd drunk any liquid as a human. Vasilije watched the sensual scene, enjoying every moment. Blood-stained lips pressed against his skin drew from him the most important gift a sire provided. As Alex swallowed every drop that spilled into his mouth, Vasilije watched his Adam's apple bob up and down in his throat. When he neared the end of the first feeding, Alex instinctively looked up to his sire to guide him.

Pulling his arm away, Vasilije let the ache in his wrist touch him inside, loving the sweet pain that accompanied feeding one of his own. Alex wiped his mouth and sat up next to him, unsure as all new vampires were.

"Come, Alex. I want to give you something."

Completely under his spell, his newest vampire followed him back to the club. Vasilije saw the brunette he'd admired earlier, without the two men she'd had before. Remembering how her body had felt against his as he'd pressed through the crowd, he approached her and with little effort, he had her nearly begging to leave with them.

By the time they arrived at his house, she had her hands all over Vasilije, but she wasn't for him.

Turning to Alex, he smiled. "She's yours for the night."

He eagerly took his gift to the couch and began undressing her. Vasilije sat back in his chair and in the dim light of the parlor, he saw his vampire bend her over and ram into her until she screamed out her orgasm. Unsatisfied, Alex pulled her head to his still hard cock and fucked her again as she eagerly swallowed everything he gave her.

Vasilije heard the familiar click of a vampire's teeth dropping as Alex came and in a flash was standing over him.

"No," he said in a deep voice like a growl.

"I'm hungry, and I know it would feel incredible to taste her now. You said she was mine."

"A vampire drinks from his sire whenever possible."

Before he could answer, Vasilije touched his wrist to Alex's mouth and the new vampire began feeding again. The brunette watched with eyes full of fear.

"Don't worry. I won't let him drink from you."

Vasilije watched the fear leave her eyes, replaced with their earlier lustful stare, now fastened on his own cock. Leaving Alex to feed, she crawled up to Vasilije and began rubbing the front of his pants. With little encouragement, she freed his cock and slid the engorged head between her lips. As her hand cupped and squeezed his balls, her mouth sucked his cock while Alex sucked excitedly at his wrist.

Looking down, Vasilije saw this was clearly not the first time this woman had sucked cock. Her tongue expertly slid under the crown, teasing the most sensitive part before she pushed her lips to gently clamp down on the base of his cock as her throat closed in around the head. The effect was incredible. Fighting the urge to come, he yanked her head off him and pulled her to her feet.

He'd said she was Alex's for the night, but now as his young vampire finished feeding for the second time in just a few hours, Alex grew sleepy, and his head fell back against the couch. The brunette looked at Alex and then back to Vasilije before she went back to work on his cock, stroking him toward completion as she softly moaned next to his lips.

"Come," he whispered.

Following him to the floor, she pulled at his clothes before he removed them with a mere thought. He ran his hands over her body slowly and then ordered, "Get on your hands and knees."

She willingly did as he commanded, and in seconds she offered him whatever he wanted. Tonight he'd take simply fucking over anything else.

Vasilije placed his hands on her hips and held her tightly in place. His cock found her drenched cunt and he slammed into her, his balls smacking off her skin. She fought against his hold, backing up to meet his hard thrusts.

Fuck, she was eager!

No matter how hard he pounded into her, she met his body's movement equally with one as wanton of her own. Vasilije slid his finger and then a second one into her ass and began fucking her in both places, and she bucked against him like she wanted more.

Roughly, he pulled her up to his chest and continued fucking her cunt. His fangs slammed into his mouth as he ran his lips over her neck.

Alex may not be able to taste her, but there was no reason he shouldn't.

He bit into her, and her moaning grew louder with each pull on her vein. The sounds of their fucking filled the room, and as he drew closer to coming, Vasilije slid his fingers down to her clit and began stroking her. His eyes closed, his mind focused on his cock filling her, his fingers teasing her, and the taste of her blood draining down his throat.

She cried out some words before she came, but he was too focused on the feel of her squeezing his cock to understand or care. Over and over, her body milked him until he filled her with his cum and she filled him with her blood.

When he finally slid out of her, she fell to the floor,

her body exhausted from how he'd treated her. Hours later, after he'd fucked her until she begged to become his, a vampire like Alex, he dissolved her memory of everything she'd done and sent her home in a cab.

As dawn approached, Vasilije made sure Alex was safe from daylight in his own bedroom designed to be secure from the sun and crawled into bed for the day. He'd had a productive night, and as he laid his head on the pillow, he smiled at how good it was to be a vampire.

2

Inch by inch, the sun slipped behind the Earth, and with each moment of night's takeover, Vasilije's body began to rouse from its slumber. As with all vampires, his very soul sensed when the sun lost its struggle to the darkness each evening, stirring his blood and awakening his hunger.

He lazily opened his eyes and stretched the day's sleep from his muscles as he turned on the light beside his bed. Slowly, the memory of the previous night washed over him, and he licked his lips to taste the last fading remnants of the brunette. He warily turned his head toward the pillow next to him, but as usual, it remained undisturbed.

As he enjoyed the memory of their time together, he heard the sound of footsteps outside his bedroom door. Jerking his head toward the sound, thoughts of the brunette were chased away by his natural predatory instincts, but after only a few moments he remembered his new vampire and let his body relax.

Alex.

Just in his second night of his new life and still in his transition period, Vasilije's new vampire would be hungrier than his sire. While he could stand a few hours of searching for the perfect victim to replace the new vampire who wasn't quite ready to feed him yet, Alex's need for blood as such a young vampire meant he was already nearly famished as he wandered the halls of Vasilije's house searching for what his body craved.

Sliding out of bed, Vasilije threw on a black silk robe over his naked body and opened the door. Outside, Alex stood staring up at him, his blue eyes wide with need.

"I'm hungry."

Vasilije welcomed him in and guided him toward the bed. Once seated, instinct took over and Alex's mouth sought out the smooth skin of his sire's wrist. For the first time, he was allowed to use his new fangs to pierce the vein, and after two failed attempts that made the ancient vampire wince in pain, Alex began to enjoy the blood of his sire.

While he fed Alex, Vasilije leisurely planned out his night in his head. Perhaps a visit to an old friend across town or a film. Better yet, a play at the theatre or a night at the opera. In a world of modern dress and manners, the theatre and opera remained perfect reminders of a time long past, a time of formal dress for men and sensual dress for women, with just enough skin to tease his lust. Compared to the almost complete nudity of the club from the night before, the theatre or opera would be just what he needed. The promise of a proper young lady giving in excited him more than any scantily clad woman at a nightclub could.

Vasilije looked down at Alex as he finished drinking

and brushed the blond hair from his face. That something forbidden that he'd desired was gone now, a casualty of the end of the chase. Now he was merely his newest vampire, a responsibility at least for the near future, but he appeared to be a quick learner, so perhaps he'd be ready for independence quicker than some of his predecessors.

The realization that once again what he'd wanted so dearly wasn't nearly as satisfying as he'd hoped disappointed him. Sighing in disgust, he gently pushed Alex's head away and closed the holes in his wrist.

Alex lay back sated, blood oozing from the corners of his mouth. His eyes rolled back into his head and he moaned in satisfaction, like a happy, contented child. After a few minutes, he rolled over and propped his head up on his hand. "What are we doing tonight, sire?"

Vasilije didn't feel like babysitting a new vampire tonight, but Alex was his responsibility, no matter how much he wanted to leave him. But that didn't mean they were going to stay in and have a slumber party in his bedroom.

Looking down into eyes that seemed incredibly innocent, far more than the night before, Vasilije said, "Tonight I'll begin to teach you how to be a vampire."

"You know, I'm not totally ignorant about the subject. I've met some before you," Alex boasted.

"Met some? Like who?"

"My girlfriend Tatiana was a vampire—is a vampire. How long before I get to go back to her? Can I at least call her?"

Vasilije stared down at Alex as he rambled on about

losing his cell phone and being lost without all his contacts. What did he mean his girlfriend is a vampire?

In need of answers and already sick of Alex's conversation, Vasilije barked, "Alex! Enough! Explain what you meant when you said your girlfriend is a vampire."

The man sat up and swung his legs over the side of the bed. "Tatiana. Yeah, she's like you. She's gonna be pissed if I don't at least call. You don't now her. She'll freak!"

Vasilije hoped he didn't know her.

Alex stood up and began looking for a phone, but Vasilije grabbed him by the arm, yanking him back onto the bed.

"Ouch! Fuck, that hurt."

"Stop sulking like a child and pay attention. I need to know. Did she ever drink from you?"

Vasilije didn't need to hear the answer. It was written all over Alex's face.

"Yeah, but it was different since she only did it when I fucked her."

Fucking great.

Vasilije closed his eyes, disgusted with himself. No wonder Alex had seemed forbidden. He was. Or he was supposed to be. He hadn't technically broken any vampire laws by claiming Alex as his, but a technicality wasn't going to help. She'd drunk from him, during sex, no less. Rightfully, he was hers.

"This Tatiana. Describe her."

"Oh man, she's hot. Tall, thin, nice tits, though. Blond hair..."

"Down to her waist," Vasilije said, finishing Alex's sentence.

"Yeah. You know her?"

Grimacing, Vasilije closed his eyes. *Yeah. He knew her.*

"Well, I have to call her. She gets pissed when I'm a couple minutes late. But just wait until she finds out I got myself made into a vampire like her. She'll be chuffed."

Vasilije moved to his closet to find clothes. Tatiana would be there any moment, and if he had to deal with a pissed off vampire, he at least wanted to be dressed for the occasion. As he slipped into black pants, he tried to explain the realities of what they'd done the night before. What he'd done.

"I wouldn't expect chuffed, Alex."

"Yeah, well she'll probably be a little torqued off that I let you when I wouldn't say yes to her, but that's okay. Now she and I can be together forever."

Vasilije pulled a red dress shirt off a hanger and slid into it. As he buttoned it, he walked over to Alex and stood in front of him. "Not exactly, Alex."

"What do you mean?"

"I'm your sire. I made you vampire. In effect, that makes you mine."

"But I can go back to Tatiana so we can be together, right?"

"No, not even if I were so inclined to let you, which I'm not."

Alex jumped up off the bed, his face red with anger. "What the fuck are you saying?"

Vasilije turned away and walked toward the door. "What I'm saying is that there won't be any more Tatiana and Alex."

"Why?" Alex asked as he hurried to catch up to his

sire, who was already making his way downstairs to await the impending arrival of Alex's ex-girlfriend.

"Because you're mine."

Vasilije knew Alex had no idea what the true implication of those words was, but Tatiana would and she wouldn't be happy.

Payback was a bitch.

"Yours? Dude, I'm not gay!" Alex continued to rant as he threw himself into a chair in frustration.

Fuck, new vampires were a handful.

"I don't mean you're mine to fuck. What being mine means is you're bound to me. If I want you here with me, then that's where you'll be. And if I let you leave, whenever I call you back, you'll come. And most of all, as your sire, I get the final say in who you're with and who you're allowed to sire."

Dumbfounded by the news that the man in front of him had almost total control of his life, Alex muttered "no" over and over as he slumped down in the chair across from Vasilije.

"Yes."

"You can't do this! She won't let you."

Vasilije knew she'd have no choice in the matter, but Tatiana wasn't going to let this go easily. He hadn't intentionally chosen her boyfriend as his newest vampire, but now that it was done, he rather liked the idea of her getting what she deserved. Or at least a small part of what she deserved.

"It's not a matter of letting me. It's done."

While Alex threatened to do things he no longer could, Vasilije summoned his butler to prepare the man for what was to come next. In just moments, the man he called Winters appeared before him and stood silently waiting for orders.

A human, Winters' name suited him perfectly. Hair as white as snow and skin to match, the tall man looked like the personification of Jack Frost. Vasilije didn't care about his looks, but his icy demeanor pleased him. His predecessor had been easily upset and prone to complaining, so Winters' somber disposition was a refreshing change.

"Winters, I'm expecting a guest tonight. When she arrives, please show her into this room."

"Shall I prepare tea, sir?"

Vasilije barely heard his butler's low voice over Alex's continual whining. "No, there's no need for that."

"Will you be needing anything else, sir?" As Winters spoke, he glanced over at Alex, who was now punctuating his speech with manic hand motions as he paced back and forth in front of the fireplace.

Vasilije seconded the irritation written all over the human's face. "No, Winters. That will be all. I'll take care of the rest."

"Yes, sir."

Winters left with one last look of disgust at Alex, and Vasilije reclined against the back of the couch in an attempt to relax before Tatiana's arrival. With tremendous effort, he blocked out Alex's protests and prepared for what he was sure would be at the very least an unpleasant scene.

Because Alex hadn't agreed to her siring him, Vasilije knew he was in the clear as far as vampire law would be concerned. It was that grey area involving her intentions toward him that presented a problem. He still believed she'd find no real sympathy with the London

Archon, but at the national realm? That was a different story. There she might be able to make some trouble for him.

But the simple truth was that as a vampire without a sire, he needed no one's permission to sire his own and wherever she took her case wouldn't be able to change that. That didn't mean this would go away easily, however.

Vasilije sensed her rage before he sensed her presence, and instantly, the pounding on the door confirmed his suspicions.

Tatiana had arrived, and she was enraged.

Winters greeted her at the door, but she pushed past him before he had the chance to make it through his prepared, "Good evening." Vasilije settled in for her fury and silently commanded Alex to join him on the couch.

Tatiana reached the parlor in seconds, and Vasilije saw just how angry she was as her green eyes flashed with rage when her gaze landed first on him and then on Alex next to him.

"I should have known it was you when I felt something last night."

"Tatiana, it's nice to see you again."

"Fuck you, Vasilije."

She turned to Alex and with one quick look Vasilije knew she saw the reality of the situation. Alex was his, and there was nothing she could do about it. Not that she wouldn't try.

"Alex, come to me, my love."

Tatiana cooed her invitation, her body's sensual positioning near him reinforcing her offer.

Vasilije felt the struggle form in Alex and silently

commanded him to remain seated. After a few moments, he gave up and sat back in defeat.

Tatiana turned to Vasilije, her rage growing by the second. "He's not yours! Let him go!"

"He is now."

Watching her fight against what she knew was true, Vasilije had to admit she was one of the most alluring women he'd ever encountered. Incredibly beautiful with long blond hair and eyes like a cat's, she possessed an allure that was undeniable. However, it was just as deadly, a fact he well knew.

"I won't let you do this. I'll take this to the Archon."

"You and your ex-boyfriend sing the same song, but you should know better."

She stood silently glaring down at him, and then slowly her face softened and her perfectly formed mouth curved into a smile. "No matter. I've drunk from him enough times to have some power of my own."

Tatiana turned to Alex and leaned in to kiss him. "My love."

Vasilije felt Alex's desire to kiss her fight against his control, but he was no match for an ancient vampire.

"Alex? Love, kiss me," she pleaded.

"I can't! He won't let me."

"While this is certainly fun, we have plans Tatiana, so I'm afraid I have to ask you to leave."

Vasilije moved to stand, but she spun toward him and pinned him to the couch. For the first time, he saw the vicious creature he'd seen all those years ago.

"I'm as powerful as you, Vasilije. I'll have you punished for this!"

Pushing her off him, Vasilije stood to face her. "For

taking your boyfriend? Have Archons taken to punishing vampires for such infractions?"

"You'd better watch, Vasilije. You have no idea what the Archons are capable of. I'll see you staked for this."

"Just what I'd expect. Like what you did to Nina."

The smile she flashed him as he said his sire's name made his stomach turn. "You didn't think I'd forgotten what you did?"

"I'm blameless in your sire's death, Vasilije."

"You may not have plunged the stake into her heart, but you're not blameless. You led that hunter to her and watched as he murdered her. One of your own. And over what? Some other pretty cock like this one?"

"You're just like your sire, Vasilije. You have no respect for other people's property. And just like her, it will get you staked."

Vasilije moved toward Tatiana and ran his fingers over her cheek. "You forget. I'm not some new vampire you're going up against. Nina was inexperienced when she sired me. I'm not. And I'm not trusting or kind like she was."

"Let me have him and none of this has to happen."

For a moment, he considered letting her have Alex, but the memory of Nina's beautiful face as she realized Tatiana had handed her over to a hunter hell bent on killing her wouldn't let him.

"No. You lose again."

In a flash, her hands were around his neck, squeezing in some futile action. Incensed, she dug her nails into the skin as she tightened her hold.

"Tatiana, you can't strangle a vampire," Vasilije said calmly.

Releasing him, she stepped back and grinned like she

knew a secret. "Remember, I gave you a chance to return him. Now I take something you cherish."

Vasilije looked over at Alex, half expecting her to try to take him as she left. He didn't cherish him, by any means, but she simply stormed out, slamming the door behind her.

"Come, Alex. It's time to go."

Still sulking, the young vampire rose and dutifully followed his sire. "Will I ever be able to return to her?"

Vasilije turned to face him, wondering how he could have chosen to sire someone so foolish.

"I love her. Please let me go to her."

Shaking his head, Vasilije answered, "No. But if you'd like, we can find that brunette again."

Alex's eyes seemed to light up and for the first time since feeding, he was happy. "The one from last night? Okay, that sounds good."

Vasilije rolled his eyes as he led Alex out into the night. "True love. How touching."

3

Sasa Lambert smoothed the bed covers across her mother's stomach as she watched her sleep for the first time in days. Only a woman in her early fifties, her mother's face, with its deep frown lines and forehead wrinkles, resembled one of a person far older. Years of living with illness had taken its toll, and along with the terrible effects of the medicine prescribed to ease her pain, the combination had left Sandra Lambert's body ravaged.

The vision of her mother finally resting brought tears to Sasa's eyes. An only child, she had taken on the responsibility for caring for her when her father left almost five years ago. Unable or unwilling to watch a woman who'd once been the beauty of the parish wither away to nothing, he left one night and simply never returned.

"Sasa? Baby?"

"Yes, Mama. I'm here."

Sasa lightly stroked her mother's cheek and brushed

the stray hairs away from her eyes. No longer the lovely chestnut brown it had once been, now her hair was steel grey and wiry, another effect of the sickness that continued its unrelenting assault on a woman who was still young in years, if not spirit.

"Baby, I'm thirsty. Can I have a drink?"

Reaching over to the nightstand, Sasa grabbed a glass of water and placed it to her mother's lips. "Drink. Slowly, Mama. Don't choke."

Water trickled down the side of her face and onto the shoulder of her nightgown. Sasa quickly found tissues and blotted her face and shoulder dry.

Her mother gently nudged her away and worked to sit up. Groaning from the pain, she finally succeeded in getting up and took the glass once again. "Thank you for not helping me, Sasa."

Standing by the bed in case her mother lost her balance, Sasa shook her head. "I hate that, Mama. That's what I'm here for."

"No. And it's not right that a beautiful girl is stuck at home with her mother. Promise me you'll go out today and have some fun."

Sasa looked down at her mother as she struggled to place the glass back on the nightstand. How could she ever go out and have fun when the person she loved more than anyone else in the world lay in bed, her body wracked with pain?

"Baby, for someone with your gift, you don't hide your feelings well."

"Mama, I can't have fun and leave you here. It's bad enough when I have to go out for just a little bit."

Her mother patted the bed next to her. "Sit. I want to talk to you."

Reluctantly, she took a seat and waited for her mother to give her the lecture she gave her at least once a week these days. Sasa didn't know why she insisted on repeating it since she'd made it quite clear many times before that she would take care of her.

"Baby, you can't go on like this. You're twenty-seven years old. By the time I was your age, I was married and had a beautiful little girl."

"It's not the same, Mama."

Sasa's mother squeezed her hand. "I know. I didn't have to take care of your mémé. But you can't let this disease take everything from you too."

Tears welled up in Sasa's eyes and began to spill out onto her cheeks. "I'm sorry, Mama. I'm just so scared."

Her mother wrapped her frail arms around her. "Let it out, baby. Let it all out."

"Oh, Mama, I can't even think about a husband and children knowing you're sick," she sobbed.

When she'd had herself a good cry—and one that was long overdue—she wiped her eyes and smiled. "Mémé would be so happy to see that. You know how she always complained that I kept my emotions all bottled up. 'That's not good for people like us, Sasa.'"

"And she's right. Who would know better than she would? An empath can't keep all those emotions in, Sasa. It's too much. You shouldn't even spend so much time near me since I'm sure my pain comes through loud and clear."

"Mama, I wouldn't care if it meant being stabbed all

over my body. I'd still be here. But it's okay. I wouldn't be much of an empath if I couldn't control how I react to other people's emotions."

Sandra Lambert brought her daughter's hand to her mouth and kissed it softly. "Baby, promise me you'll go out today. Find some old friends. Make some new ones. Promise me."

Too tired to argue with her, Sasa nodded. "Yes, Mama. I promise."

"Good. I'm tired now. I'm going to take a little nap."

Sasa kissed her mother's cheek. "Sleep well. I'll be back in a little while after I run my errand."

Her mother rolled over away from her, and Sasa waited until she was sure she was asleep before quietly slipping out. The errand she had to run wasn't one she could ever tell her mother about, or anyone else, for that matter. But that didn't stop her from going where she had to.

SASA STOOD on the sidewalk of Iberville Street hesitating for just a moment before she entered Madame Quiterie's. One of a variety of voodoo and alternative healing shops in New Orleans, it was owned by a Haitian woman who claimed to be a voodoo priestess.

The bell above the door announced her arrival, and Sasa looked around the dimly lit shop but saw no one. Quiterie's text had said she needed to see her at six o'clock, but the shop seemed empty.

"Quiterie! You here?"

Silence.

Unwilling to risk angering her, Sasa browsed the store

while she waited. She'd lived in New Orleans long enough to doubt that most of Madame Quiterie's merchandise did anything truly mystical. Much of it looked like fodder for gullible tourists curious about voodoo but ignorant to its meaning. Fake stones and supposedly enchanted trinkets she was sure were made in China sat in baskets along the dingy shop's shelves. Near the register were herbs of all kinds in little oddly shaped bottles that looked like teardrops.

Sasa popped the cork on one labeled Wormwood and lifted the bottle to her nose.

"You want to be careful with that, baby."

Spinning around, she saw Quiterie standing in the doorway to the back office. "Really? This is dangerous?"

"Pure wormwood oil is very dangerous. Interested in making a deal with the devil?"

Sasa quickly replaced the cork in the bottle and put it back with the others. "What do you mean?"

"Wormwood is used in spells to make a pact with the devil."

Sasa looked down at the basket of bottles and back at Quiterie. "Oh. No, no. You said you needed to see me in your text?"

"Yes. I have something I need you to do for me."

Sasa had to admit she already felt like she'd made a deal with the devil. Six months earlier, in a moment of desperation over her mother, she'd come to Quiterie to find something that could give her at least some relief. Quiterie had taken pity on her and performed a spell to cure her mother. She'd never believed it would cure the disease, but when her mother improved, she was hooked.

Since then, whenever her health got worse, Sasa

returned to ask for more spells—protection, health, well-being—whatever worked. But Madame Quiterie didn't work cheaply and quickly Sasa needed more spells but had no money to pay.

So she told her about her gift.

Quiterie was nothing if not an enterprising woman, a fact Sasa soon realized. Instead of making Sasa pay for her services to help her mother, she offered to be paid in trade. Any time the voodoo priestess needed a bit more "insight", as she called it, into a client or a situation, she called on Sasa. Usually it was just minor work, like sensing a client's emotions during a tarot reading. She'd sit hidden behind the person and signal to Quiterie to let her know she was affecting them one way or another. It had all the grace of a carnival side show, but if it meant her mother suffered less, then Sasa could swallow her pride.

"I have someone coming in today. Same as always. Come into the office and I'll tell you about it."

Sasa followed her into the dimly lit room and sat down on the other side of the desk from the woman. Through the haze of incense, she looked at her partner in crime, or at least in deceit. Quiterie looked every bit the part of New Orleans voodoo priestess. A striking woman, she had big brown eyes that seemed so full of emotion all the time. Sasa found this ironic since she'd never once picked up any real emotions from her. It was as if she were an empty shell.

Her dark skin remained unlined, even though Sasa was sure Quiterie was closer to her mother's age than hers. What her hair looked like she couldn't say. She'd never seen even a wisp of it escape from the brightly colored scarves she always wore and which always matched her long, flowing dresses that hid her more than ample figure.

"The client I have coming in today, dear, I need a clear read on. As clear as you can give me."

"That's fine. Anything else I can know about this person beforehand?"

Quiterie didn't answer for a long moment and then when she did, she sounded more mysterious than Sasa had ever heard her be.

"She's from far away and is looking for something very unique."

"Okay." That didn't really tell her anything, but that was probably a good thing. She didn't need to be any deeper in a voodoo priestess's business than she already was.

"When is she getting here?"

"I expect her any minute, so take your place."

Sasa hurried behind the curtain near the door and waited. As she sat there, she made a mental list of the things she hoped to get done after she finished playing Wizard of Oz for Quiterie. Hopefully, her mother was still napping so she'd have time to cook the rest of the week's dinners when she got home.

The ring of the front doorbell shook her from her planning, and she pressed her eye to a hole in the black curtain to see Madame Quiterie's mystery client. With her face against the scratchy cloth, she saw the woman was tall with long blond hair. She wore all black, which accentuated how thin she was and made her seem even taller. It also gave her an ominous air.

She had an English accent and spoke formally, as if

she were an actress playing a part from the 1800s. For a moment, Sasa got lost in her voice and its almost hypnotic quality, but Quiterie's voice saying the word she always used to remind her to pay attention brought her back to focus.

"Welcome my dear. Tell me what you've come to Madame Quiterie's for today, dear."

Two dears was her signal for Sasa to begin.

"I want your help to exact revenge on someone."

Sasa sat up straighter on the wooden stool, suddenly interested in this client. Most of Quiterie's customers came looking for spells to make someone fall in love with them or to help them win millions in the lottery. Those people were easy to sense. They were desperate. Even Quiterie could sense that.

Then there were those that were a little darker, like the women who wanted help breaking up a marriage to have the man of their dreams. It was this type of person Sasa was there to read. Not necessarily desperate, these clients were the kind that Quiterie wanted to string along. They had definite goals and given the right emotional manipulation, could be convinced of any measure of success, even where there was none.

This woman was exactly the kind of client Quiterie liked.

"Revenge? What kind of revenge are you looking for, my dear?"

Yes—why would a woman like this need a voodoo priestess to get revenge on someone?

Sasa closed her eyes and opened herself up to the emotions radiating from the blond next to Quiterie. Her formal way of speech and proper English accent masked a firestorm of feelings, which instantly threatened to overwhelm Sasa. Never before had she sensed such rage and hatred in another. The level of sheer anger coming from her frightened Sasa, and for the first time in her arrangement with Quiterie, she wanted to run.

"I want him dead, but first I need him to suffer."

"Dead?"

Oh, my God! Had she really said that out loud?

Before Sasa could escape, the blond had ripped the curtain from in front of her and stood glaring down at her with her green eyes full of rage.

"Is this some kind of sham, Madame Quiterie? What's going on here?"

Sasa stood from her stool, speechless and waiting for Quiterie to give an explanation for why she'd been hiding there. Her growing fear exploded into terror when the blond opened her mouth and with a sharp click flashed two white fangs. Quiterie's client was a vampire!

"No, no! No sham! Please let me introduce my helper, Sasa Lambert."

"Sasa." The blond said her name as if it were a curse.

"Sasa has a very unique gift. Tell her Sasa."

Hesitating at first, Sasa finally uttered, "I'm...I'm an empath."

"She can sense people's emotions. I'd say that's a very useful gift, wouldn't you?"

"People's emotions? What about mine? Can you sense mine, Sasa?"

Timidly, she answered, "Yes."

Sasa glanced over at Quiterie, unsure of how much to

say, but she saw her nod to give her the go-ahead and looked back at the blond.

"I can feel the anger pouring off you. Whoever got you angry, he's made an enemy in you, for sure."

"Very true. You'll do fine."

"Do?"

Quiterie spoke up. "Sasa, Tatiana needs you to use your gift to help her."

Forgetting that the blond still flashed fangs, Sasa stepped past her toward Quiterie's desk. "No. I can't do that. I won't."

"You want me to keep helping your mama, don't you, Sasa?"

Sasa felt like someone had kicked her in the stomach. What if Quiterie didn't continue her spells for her mother? She couldn't let her suffer like that.

"I can't help you kill someone. Even my mother's health isn't enough to make me do that."

Sasa knew very little about vampires, other than they obviously existed and they didn't suffer from disease. Or at least that's what she'd heard. An idea crept into her mind and without thinking it through, Sasa turned toward Tatiana. "But I'll help you if you help my mother."

"And just what do you want me to do with your mother?"

"Make her like you—a vampire."

Tatiana's face registered her surprise at Sasa's request. When she didn't answer, Sasa was sure she'd lost the standoff, but just as she was about to agree to help in exchange for more of Quiterie's spells, Tatiana spoke again.

"Fine. I will sire your mother. Is this your only demand, empath?"

Sasa didn't believe it was in her best interest to ask for anything else, but she did need to know what she would do to her mother. "What will happen to her? Will she feel any pain?"

"Why do you want your mother to be a vampire?"

Sasa's chest tightened at the thought of her mother. "My mother's sick. She's always in pain. I don't want her to have to deal with more."

Tatiana smiled. "After I sire her, she'll be as healthy as a horse, as long as you give her the blood I give you to help her through her first days as a vampire."

"Is that it? What about after that?"

"That's what people are for."

"Then we have a deal? I'll help you and you'll help my mother?"

Tatiana grinned wide enough so Sasa could see her fangs again. "Deal, empath. We need to go now, though."

Quiterie stood surprised and disappointed, Sasa thought, since now that Tatiana would make her mother a vampire, she wouldn't need any more of the voodoo priestess's spells.

"Tatiana, let me know if you need anything else."

Sasa looked at both women and had the surest sense they were keeping something from her. Just as Tatiana made it to the door, Sasa said, "First my mother. Then I help you."

She wasn't sure, but she could have sworn the woman growled before turning around.

"Fine. Let's go."

Sasa hurried to catch up with Tatiana, not knowing if

she'd just made the biggest mistake of her life or the best choice available to cure her mother's misery. Worse, she had no reason to believe her deal with the vampire was anything more than her serving herself and her mother up as Tatiana's next two-course meal.

But if there was a chance to save her mother, she had to take it.

4

Vasilije stretched out across his bed, enjoying an early night in. Weeks of training Alex had been taxing, but he was finally ready to be left on his own. He'd chosen to go out earlier, and Vasilije was thankful for the peace and quiet.

Alex had developed the habit of picking up women each night and had all but forgotten his feelings for Tatiana, so he could be trusted alone. That he acted like a horny schoolboy had become tiresome, but Vasilije was happy that his obviously deep love for Tatiana was no longer an issue.

The overriding boredom Vasilije felt was another thing entirely. That wouldn't go away as easily as Alex's feelings of love. Centuries of siring vampires who quickly became a duty more than anything else made him yearn for excitement.

"Maybe a visit somewhere warm," he muttered into the silence of his room.

Years of the commonplace left him with an unfulfilled
need, one that couldn't be satisfied with anything he
could find at his usual haunts. How had life become so
mundane?

As he began to slip into self-pity, suddenly a pain
stabbed at his chest, and he sat bolt upright in the dark
clutching near his heart. One of his vampires had just left
his life. Who? Where?

Vasilije's heart raced in terror as his mind searched
for the spirit of each vampire he'd sired. One by one, he
located each of them....and then nothing. Desperately, he
reached out to Teagan, one he hadn't seen since he'd left
for America six years ago, but felt his life slip away until
only a void remained.

Blind with rage, Vasilije threw on his clothes and in
minutes was ready to begin looking for the bastard who'd
killed one of his own. When he found them, they'd beg
for him to do as they'd done to Teagan.

He wouldn't be that merciful.

VASILIJE LOOKED around the room he'd just appeared in,
his body alert to any danger. He'd followed the sense he'd
gotten before Teagan's spirit had been extinguished and
knew he was in his home in New Orleans. Everything
about the place was Teagan—from the Turkish cigarettes
he smoked, to the bottle of Guinness that sat on the
coffee table, to the musky scent that identified him as one
of Vasilije's vampires.

And the beautiful woman staring at him.

"Who did this?" Vasilije demanded.

Big brown eyes stared back at him. "I don't know. It

happened so fast. I left to grab another six pack and when I got back, someone had a stake..."

Vasilije stood watching the stranger as she cried, needing more information but forced to wait until there was a break in her tears.

"Who are you?"

The woman dried her eyes and sniffled. "Sasa. I was his girlfriend."

At the use of the past tense, she began tearing up again, but Vasilije didn't have time for it. Whoever had staked Teagan couldn't have gone too far and any more time wasted with Sasa's crying may mean he'd lose the fucker.

He moved to leave, and her hand caught his arm.

"Please don't go."

She looked up at him with such a sad expression for a moment he didn't want to go. But he couldn't let Teagan's murderer escape. Vasilije touched his hand to hers to remove it from his arm, but all this did was make her squeeze tighter.

"Please," she begged in a voice that matched the pathetic look in her eyes. "Don't leave me alone now."

The urge to tear his arm from her hold and leave her to her misery spiked in him, but it was overruled by that small part of him that understood her sadness.

"Fine. Follow me. And keep up. And if I tell you to do something, do it. Do you understand?"

For a second, she looked surprised, and Vasilije thought he was going to hear a string of irritating questions. None came, though, and when he turned to head out the door, she followed silently.

At the street, he stopped and inhaled deeply, hoping

to sense something that would help him find Teagan's killer. Nothing came. But there'd been something in the apartment...something that he was sure he recognized.

Eyes closed, he let his other senses take over, but he got nothing. "What did he look like?"

"I don't know. It was so quick. Blond, I think."

Vasilije snapped his head to the left to look at her. "Man or woman?"

Instantly, Tatiana's threat repeated in his head. *Now I take something you cherish.* Had she staked one of his vampires in retaliation over Alex? Vasilije doubted even Tatiana would stake a vampire herself, but she wasn't above having someone else do it.

"Man."

That didn't mean Tatiana wasn't behind Teagan's murder. And who was this woman who claimed to be Teagan's girlfriend?

"Did you see which direction he ran?"

Sasa shook her head sadly. "No, I'm sorry. Are you his sire?"

"How do you know about that?" he asked, more suspicious than he'd been just a minute earlier.

"Teagan was a vampire, and you just look like a sire would. That's what you call them, right?"

As she spoke, Vasilije studied her under the streetlight's glow, still unsure she was who she claimed to be. Not bad looking, she seemed like someone Teagan could like. He'd always preferred brunettes with big eyes and bigger tits, and although she didn't measure up to porn star level, she still had a nice body. He could see her as Teagan's girlfriend.

"Yeah, I'm his sire and right now I need to find the

fuck who killed one of my vampires," he said looking down the street.

"What's your name?"

Turning to look at her, he raised one eyebrow. "You're a curious one, aren't you, pet?"

"Well, I think I should know your name if we're going to work together to find Teagan's killer."

Vasilije continued to work on getting any sense of who he was looking for, but nothing came to him. Frustrated, he'd need time to think and find his way around this new place before he could search for the killer, and the last thing he needed was a weepy woman tagging along.

"Uh, no. We're not going to be working together to find anything. Just point me to the nearest place I can get something to eat, and I'll be on my way."

In a second, her hands were back on his arm and squeezing. "Please let me help. I want to see the person who did this brought to justice."

Justice? Vasilije smiled at the idea of justice, sure she would be appalled by what he intended to do to Teagan's killer. Humans were always more squeamish than he thought they should be, considering their own history.

"How long were you and Teagan together?"

"Why?"

Vasilije noticed her defensiveness immediately. Her body language screamed she was hiding something.

"You just seem very attached. That's all."

Sasa shifted her weight between her feet. "I was. I mean, we were. Attached. And even though we had problems, we were trying to work things out."

"Problems?"

A sheepish look came over her face. "I forgave him, and we'd have worked things out..."

Sasa's lip quivered for just a second, and Vasilije was afraid she'd begin crying again. Teagan hadn't changed in his new home, it seemed. A notorious ladies' man, his wandering eye had been the reason he'd moved four thousand miles away from the only place he'd ever called home. Obviously, that relationship hadn't survived since Sasa stood next to him all dewy eyed over his death.

"I see."

"It's not like that. It doesn't matter what you think anyway. I just owe it to him to find out who did this."

Vasilije smiled at Sasa's words. She was probably completely unaware that the one she'd caught her boyfriend with was likely one of many. Such blind devotion.

"Love, I don't think you understand what's going to happen when I find the guy who did this. My idea of justice and yours aren't the same, I guarantee you."

Sasa's eyes grew wide. "Why? Is there some kind of ritual you plan to perform when you punish him?"

Vasilije's fangs snapped into position, and he grinned to show her the weapons he'd use to punish the mother-fucker who killed one of his own.

"No ritual. Just these and all the blood I can handle."

The shock at his words was written all over her face. "You plan to drain them?"

"My kind of justice, love. So if you plan to stick around, you know what to expect."

Sure he'd frightened her enough to change her mind, he began walking toward the nearest main road. Before he could begin searching for Teagan's killer, he had to find something to eat. Then he'd use Teagan's house since it would be set up for someone like him and work out of there.

"Will you bite me?"

Vasilije turned to look at her standing there staring at him, the fear gone from her eyes, replaced by something he couldn't quite put his finger on.

Curiosity? Desire?

"Only if you want me to, love."

As if she'd expected him to say yes and when she heard a different answer her mind instantly moved on to something else, Sasa marched past him, waving him on to follow her.

"Follow me. I'll take you where you can get something to eat and I can get a drink."

Vasilije grimaced at the idea that this stray woman was now giving him orders. He should have gone with his first instinct and left her. Maybe Teagan had cared for her, though, and would want her to help him. He owed him at least that much.

———

SASA'S LEGS shook so violently she was sure the large vampire behind her would hear her knees knock and become suspicious of her. In one night, she'd been foolish enough to become involved with not just one but two vampires. Three if the one she'd watched murdered was counted. And she couldn't decide which one was more frightening.

As she questioned whether she'd finally lost her mind, she remembered the man following her hadn't given her his name. Spinning around, she asked as casually as she could muster, "So what's your name?"

Her heart skipped a beat when he stepped close to her and said in a deep voice, "Vasilije. And I'm hungry."

She genuinely hoped he meant for food, especially since she thought she saw him eyeing up her neck.

He walked past her, giving her a chance to thoroughly check him out from behind. The front view had been stunning, albeit frightening. His black hair was straight and glossy with stray strands that fell into his eyes. She imagined it would feel incredible between her fingers, like strands of the darkest silk sliding over her skin.

Then there were his eyes. Crystal blue, they were cold and expressive at the same time.

But the most frightening part of him was his mouth, and he knew it. Unlike Tatiana's, whose fangs sounded more ominous than they looked, Vasilije's fangs looked razor-sharp, like a wild animal's. She'd noticed Teagan's were similar and wondered if a vampire's sex had anything to do with their fangs' sharpness.

Poor Teagan! She'd had no idea Tatiana meant to kill him when she followed her to his house. She'd ranted on about this one all the way there, but when she'd called Teagan by name, Sasa had thought perhaps she'd been spared the sight of Tatiana killing someone tonight.

What have I gotten myself into?

"Love, you're supposed to be leading the way. Stop daydreaming and take me to some food."

"I'm sorry. I was just thinking about..."

Sasa let her sentence trail off, sure by the look of

disgust on Vasilije's face that he wouldn't ask about what she was thinking. Catching up to him, she hoped she wouldn't have to pretend to be the sad girlfriend much more. As it was, she was giving an Oscar-worthy performance, but she had to be careful not to overplay her role. If this vampire found out she was working for Tatiana, something told her she'd know instantly who was more frightening. He might look like the most erotic dream a woman may have, but she was sure angered he'd quickly become her worst nightmare.

Sasa led him to a side street off Teagan's street and a little hole-in-the-wall bar called Napoleon's. She'd been there once with the boyfriend she'd used as material when she'd told Vasilije of her problems with Teagan and remembered it being secluded. Perfect for a discreet drink with a vampire.

He stood for a moment eyeing the sign and turned to her. "Original for these parts?"

She couldn't help but smile as she opened the screen door to enter. To locals, the idea of a place being named Napoleon's seemed perfectly natural, but to an outsider, she knew it must have seemed almost campy.

"It's a local thing."

In a voice as sarcastic as he'd used for his last comment, he remarked, "I guess the thought is if it works once, it will work every other time?"

Sasa walked directly to the darkest booth and slid in followed by Vasilije. The fixture on the wall next to them threw little light, and for the first time that night, she relaxed despite the fact that he was staring at her. She tried to sense his emotions, but for the most part, all she felt was irritation.

"You said your name was Sasa, right?"

"Yes."

"Okay. Well, Sasa, something tells me this isn't a place with waitresses, so tell me what's good to eat here and I'll go tell that man behind the bar."

"Po-boys are really good. So are the crawfish. Do you know what they are?"

"No. Why don't you tell me what Teagan liked and I'll go from there."

Sasa's stomach clenched, and she scrambled to think of what to say. All she'd known of his dead friend was he'd had an English accent.

"Po-boys. Shrimp po-boys. He loved them."

Nodding, Vasilije said, "Then a po-boy it is. What do you want?"

"Oh, nothing to eat. Just get me a beer. A light beer." Reaching into her purse, she pulled out a twenty. "Here, in case you don't have money."

Vasilije walked to the bar, and Sasa's gaze followed him. Dressed in black pants and what looked like a shirt meant to be worn with a suit, his body filled out both nicely. Where was he from? He didn't have an accent like Tatiana or Teagan, but he definitely sounded foreign.

As she waited for him to return, Sasa's mind drifted back to her mother. Tatiana had done as she'd promised and made her into one of them. For the first time in years, she felt good. That she was horrified about what Sasa had done bothered her, but she'd forgive her some day. What mattered was that she was no longer in pain and able to leave the bed she'd stayed in for so many years. She'd see that someday. For now, she was at her cousin's house with the blood Tatiana had given her, and

Sasa silently prayed to God everything would be all right.

As silent as a cat, Vasilije slid back into the booth and sat back once again to stare at her. "The man behind the bar says my food will be ready soon. There's your change and your beer."

Sasa was thankful for the drink. If she ever needed a drink, it was now. She quickly emptied the glass and rose to get another. "Do you want one?"

"Scotch. Rocks."

After a few minutes at the bar, Sasa returned with their drinks and his food. As he ate, they sat in silence, something she was thankful for. Every sentence she uttered was another chance she'd say the wrong thing and expose what she was doing. If she could steer all their conversations toward general topics, that would be great, but as she watched Vasilije finish his first taste of southern food, she doubted he was much for sports or movies, the two topics she knew she could handle easily.

When he finished, he sat back against the booth. "Thank you, Sasa. That was surprisingly good. No wonder Teagan enjoyed them so much."

"I'm glad you liked it, although I don't think I've ever seen anyone eat a po-boy with a scotch," she said with a chuckle.

"I'm sure."

Sasa finished her second beer and stood to return to the bar. "You want another?"

"No, thanks."

By the time she'd finished two more beers, she was feeling more relaxed than she'd been in years. She knew she was supposed to be helping Tatiana, but as they sat together in that dark booth, she began to sense the sadness Vasilije felt at the loss of Teagan.

The words "I'm sorry" sat on the tip of her tongue, and she so wished she could comfort the man who sat across from her.

5

Vasilije was thankful Teagan's girlfriend remained silent, allowing him the chance to reminisce on the last time he'd seen him. Six years had gone by in a flash, and it seemed like only yesterday he'd been in his parlor making his case for a move to America.

No matter how many times he'd gone through the loss of one of his vampires, Vasilije never got used to it. Never got used to the feeling that a piece of him had been cut out, lost forever. Never got used to the sadness that mingled with rage and threatened to take him over.

It was a potent combination that made his insides churn. Like every time in the past, he'd be forced to walk a fine line between mourning and unremitting anger until he found the one responsible. When he did, he'd willingly allow his emotions to control him to punish the man.

Until then, however, he needed to stuff down both the sadness and the anger if he wanted to function.

Lost in his thoughts, Vasilije hadn't noticed Sasa had

downed two more beers and now seemed a different person. The bar had begun to fill up, and he smelled desire coming off the men around them toward the only female in the bar.

"Sasa, it's time to go," he said as he stood to leave. "Take my arm."

A confused look settled onto her face. "Oh, okay. Why?"

"Just do it, love."

Sasa took his arm and Vasilije felt the tension in the bar dissipate as those around them understood she was protected. He wouldn't mind releasing some of his own tension on anyone who pissed him off, but for now he'd prefer leaving without the hassle of a fight.

Once outside, Vasilije attempted to take his arm back, but she held fast to it and leaned her head on his upper arm. "What made you think I was in danger in there?"

"How do you know I didn't just want you close?" he joked.

They walked for a few blocks and finally she answered, "You seem like the type of man who'd handle that smoother."

Vasilije looked down at her head resting against him. She was drunk. And she was Teagan's girlfriend. Doing anything like what he was thinking would be taking advantage of her.

As he worked to convince himself that sleeping with someone who'd just lost her boyfriend only hours earlier was shitty, he didn't realize they'd made their way back to Teagan's house and were already at the front steps.

"Sasa, I should've taken you home."

All she did was shake her head and squeeze his arm.

. . .

VASILIJE DIDN'T BOTHER to turn the lights on once inside. In truth, as a vampire, he saw as well in the dark as humans did in the light. Even more, there was no point in acting like they were going to sit on the couch and talk or watch television.

He knew what she wanted and he wanted it too.

Closing the door behind him, he reached out to her and pulled her to him, enjoying the feel of her body pressed to his. She was so warm. So willing.

Her hands slid over his stomach and chest as she arched up to kiss him. Bending down, his lips grazed hers for a moment before he pulled her closer, wanting what she offered.

Warm and wet, her mouth eagerly pressed against his and her tongue met his, teasing him with the tip. His fangs had slid into his mouth at the first touch of her hands on his body, and each playful flick of her tongue came so close, just missing them. To feel her tongue against his fangs would be heaven.

His hand tightened its grip in her hair and tugged, making her moan into his mouth. God, he wanted to hear that sound again. The sound of a woman needy for everything he could give her.

Sasa slid her hands over his shoulders and pulled him to her, pressing her breasts against his body as she devoured his mouth. Her tightened nipples rubbed against him, exciting him. Instinctively, he slid his hand under her thin t-shirt and plucked at one hardened pearl through her lacy bra, squeezing it gently between his thumb and forefinger as he cupped the fullness surrounding it.

Again, she moaned, making that sound that hit him

directly between his legs. Already rock hard, his cock strained against the front of his pants. Whatever his mind may have thought about sleeping with her, his body had different plans.

And then her tongue flicked over the tip of one fang and sensations raced from his balls, up his cock, and through his body.

"Fuck," he groaned as she seductively slid her tongue over his fang again. She had to know what she was doing to him. She had been a vampire's girlfriend.

The idea that he was about to fuck the girlfriend of his dead vampire momentarily made Vasilije pull back from her, but the touch of her hands on his stomach made him forget every guilty feeling he had. Looking down, he watched her fumble with the shirt buttons.

"Sasa."

At the sound of her name, she looked up and even in the darkness he saw the look of desire on her face. In one swift movement, he pinned her hands above her head. Pushing her up against the wall, he leaned into her and pressed his thigh between her legs, feeling the heat coming from her. Slowly, a low growl slid from his throat.

Sasa pushed against his hands, but he wouldn't release her. Grinding against his thigh, she arched her body toward his.

His free hand lifted her shirt over her head and in seconds she stood before him in only her bra. A quick flick with his fingers and it was sailing to the floor to join her shirt.

Vasilije cupped one supple breast in his hand and tenderly stroked her silky soft flesh with his fingertips. Eager to feel her on his tongue, he bent his head and captured a nipple, quickly sucking it to an excited peak. A moan drew his attention from her tightened pink nipple, and he looked up to see Sasa's face. Brown eyes clouded over with need stared into his.

"Please let me touch you. I want to feel you."

Silently, he released her hands and returned to what his mouth craved. She felt so good in his mouth. Each pull made her grind her pussy against his thigh. Her hands raked through his hair, stroking and tugging as he sensually nibbled on her.

Vasilije couldn't remember when he'd been with a woman who was so responsive. Every spot his mouth and hands visited aroused her, and she seemed to worship his body as she moved her hands from his hair to caress his neck and shoulders through his shirt.

Softly, he grazed her nipple with his fangs and from above he heard her cry out. He stood up and smiled with satisfaction, his sharp fangs aching to sink into her. He was surprised to find not fear in her face but desire—pure desire. Her cry hadn't been of pain but pleasure.

Was she just drunk, or did she realize what he planned to do?

As he studied her in the darkness, she pulled him to her and kissed him with a need that sent a jolt to his cock. His hands made their way to her jeans, and he made quick work of the button and zipper. Only cotton panties stood between him and his goal.

Vasilije slid two fingers under those panties and down through her bare slickness. Sasa wriggled against his hand as her mouth fed on his, her tongue darting in and around the inside passionately.

Bending down to pull her pants off, he whispered in

her ear, "Careful, love. Teagan may have been able to control himself when you toyed with his fangs, but I won't."

Sasa stood in front of him naked and looking up at him as she licked her lips. Lifting herself onto her toes, she whispered next to his mouth, "You mean like this?" and then slowly ran her tongue over the point of his left fang.

His head thrown back, one thought controlled him now.

SASA WASN'T sure what he meant about his fangs, but she was sure she'd never felt anything like the emotions coming off him. Powerful. Sensual.

She loved the idea that she might be the reason for how he felt. She'd been with other men who'd said she did it for them, but their emotions had always told a different story. Even with Jason, who she knew had truly loved her, she'd never felt anything like what Vasilije was feeling.

In a flash, her back was against the wall and she was lifted off the ground. His strong hands held her tightly as he pushed close to her.

"Don't say I didn't warn you," he growled close to her ear.

In the blink of an eye, his clothes vanished and his naked body, hard and powerful, pressed against her body. She knew she should be frightened. He was a vampire and the words he'd just said were tinged with more than a hint of a threat. She'd felt how sharp his fangs were—

fangs that could plunge into her as he proceeded to drink every last drop of her blood and kill her.

She didn't care.

Desperate to have him inside her, she pulled his mouth to hers and flicked her tongue again over the tip of one fang. In the dark, she was blind to his reaction, but every other sense screamed to her that she wouldn't have to wait a second longer for him to give her what she craved.

With no warning, he thrust into her, filling the empty space completely and taking her breath away. He poured every emotion he had into her—all the rage and sadness at losing Teagan, all the desire and need to have her. With each thrust, it all came pouring out of him.

Sasa held onto his neck, her fingers passionately tugging on his hair, just as soft as she'd imagined. Her legs held him tight around his waist, pulling him closer each time he reared back to plunge into her.

Lost in the sensual rhythm of his fucking, she slowly realized the deep growl he made as he moved his mouth to her neck. From somewhere deep inside him, he groaned her name.

"Sasa."

His voice sounded full of every emotion she was experiencing. But at its core wasn't rage or lust but sadness. She wanted to make that sadness disappear. For just a few moments, make him forget his loss like he made her forget the loneliness that had been part of every fiber of her being for so long.

Sasa cradled his head in her arms, feeling the scrape of those razor-sharp teeth on her neck. Could she let him do that like she'd let Tatiana do to her mother? Fear bubbled up inside her. Would he take everything from her and leave her empty and for dead?

Almost on their own, the words left her mouth. "Please don't hurt me."

Vasilije stopped and lifted his head from her neck. How much she wished she could see his face! With each second that ticked by, she wondered if she'd die there because of what she'd said, in some strange man's house, a just ending for what had happened there only hours earlier.

He remained silent in front of her, his lips close enough that she felt his warm breath brush her cheek. She had no idea how long they stayed like that, him still inside her, holding her to him, before he carried her to the couch and gently lifted her off him.

Alone on the couch, Sasa felt cold lying there without him, but then he lowered his body down to meet hers and whispered against her lips, "I won't take what you won't willingly give."

A sigh of relief escaped her mouth just as he pressed his lips to hers, softly and almost reverently. The fear that had just been racing through her vanished, replaced by the need to willingly offer him the one thing she desperately yearned to give. Herself.

Again, he slid into her joining them as one, but he was different now. Sasa felt a gentleness from him as what had begun as something raw eased into something sweeter shared between the two of them.

Her hands stroked the soft skin of his back, up and down from the tightened muscles just above his waist to the space between his broad shoulders. His body felt like a silken piece of art under her fingertips. With every thrust into her welcoming body, she worshipped him with her hands.

He seemed driven by one desire—the need to please her. All she felt from him now was sweetness, like a form of love felt when one finds acceptance in another. Sasa knew it wasn't the type of love found in tender love songs. She wasn't a fool. He barely knew her, and this was the result of too much alcohol and his need for the closeness of someone, anyone, to take away the pain of losing his friend.

In some ways, though, it was so much more than the melodramatic love of songs. For so long, she'd devoted herself to taking care of her mother that her happiness had all but been forgotten. Loneliness had become who she was. She sensed that whatever his life had been before coming here that it had had its fair share of loneliness too. For this night, at least, each of them had someone to share themselves with to chase away the solitude of their lives.

Slowly, her body began to surrender to the physical pleasure he gave. Somewhere deep inside, she became alive again.

"Yes...right there...don't stop," she begged as she held him tightly to her.

Vasilije's deep voice was in her ear willing her body to do what he wished and it desperately yearned for. "Come for me, Sasa."

As he spoke her name, she tumbled over the edge that marked her surrender. Over and over, her body milked his cock through her orgasm as the most delicious sensations raced through every inch of her. Without thinking, she raked her nails over his smooth back, sinking into the corded muscles as she rode out each wonderful spasm.

She felt his climax as his stomach tightened against hers and moaned his name as a plea to join her in her ecstasy. A moment later, he stilled as he spent himself inside her, his panting the only sound in her ears.

They lay silently entwined in one another's arms for a long time, as Sasa listened to his soft breathing near her ear and felt his heartbeat next to her chest gradually slow. Vasilije made no movement toward leaving her body, not that she wanted him to, but as the minutes passed, she wished he'd say something. His emotions told her he was happy, but his silence confused her.

Finally, she whispered his name and hoped he hadn't fallen asleep.

"Sasa," he answered in a contented voice.

His answer was as confusing as his silence. She wanted more than ever before not to break the spell of incredible sex, but now she suddenly felt self-conscious about sleeping with him.

"I should go," she abruptly announced, awkwardly breaking the silence.

"Don't."

Of all the words that could have come out of his mouth, that was possibly the one that thrilled her the most. Relieved that his silence hadn't been a signal of his regret, she relaxed and playfully asked, "Then can we change positions so you can be on the bottom?"

Kissing her, he stood up and took her hand in his to pull her upright on the couch. "Better?"

"Much. Thank you."

Sasa began to say something else, but instead of

taking a seat next to her, she heard him walk away in the pitch darkness, never running into anything as he made his way to the kitchen. Then he was next to her on the couch, lighting a candle on the table in front of them.

"You don't say much, do you?"

Vasilije turned his head to look at her and smiled. In the flicker of the candlelight, she saw for the first time how blue his eyes were, how they sparkled now when he looked at her.

Leaning back, he pulled her to him, resting her head on his chest. As his heart gently beat in her ear, she asked, "What kind of name is Vasilije?"

Teasing, he answered, "What kind of name is Sasa?"

"I asked first."

"Romanian."

"So you're Romanian? Is that your accent?"

He remained quiet for a long moment and finally in a tone far more serious said, "I am vampire. Nothing more."

6

By the time Vasilije awoke, Sasa was gone. As the sleep left his eyes, he turned and looked next to him. The pillow still held the indentation where she'd placed her head when she'd finally rolled off him just before they'd fallen asleep together.

Looking around the room, he saw signs of Teagan everywhere. His books resting on the shelf. His clothes hanging in the closet. More of those goddamned Turkish cigarettes that always stunk so much. The sadness he'd felt yesterday came rushing back and slowly morphed into a sharpened rage by the time he set out to begin the search for his killer almost an hour later.

God, he felt like shit! The thought of Teagan being staked was bad enough, but the possibility that his death was payback for his siring Alex was almost torture. His hands balled into tight fists as he made his way toward the French Quarter.

What he needed now was a drink, but even more he needed to feed. As much as he'd wanted to taste Sasa, his promise to not take her against her will was one he intended to keep.

Something about her gnawed at him still. He hadn't planned on sleeping with her. That it happened was just something between two people lonely after a loss. At least that's what he'd told himself when he'd begun to kiss her. And then when he'd nearly lost his mind when she'd played with his fangs, almost sending him over the edge. And again when he was inside her feeling more at home and happy with a woman than he had been in a long time.

As he crossed Canal Street into the Quarter, he shook his head trying to get her out of his mind. He had other things he had to deal with, and a woman wasn't really one he had the time for.

Vasilije stepped into the mob of people heading toward Bourbon Street and let the feeling of the crowd wash over him. As he passed a restaurant, the fragrant smell of Cajun spices hit his nose and mingled with the earthy aroma of the humans surrounding him, producing a distinct scent he'd never smelled anywhere else in the world. The need for blood rose up in him, and his body began to ache.

Eyeing the row of bars, he stood amazed at the sight in front of him. Neon greens, yellows, and oranges danced in front of his eyes as beacons calling him to visit. It was as if the universe had sensed his craving and laid out a banquet just for him. People danced on balconies above him, shouting their excitement down to the street below. Never before, even in London, had he sensed a city so alive. Inhaling deeply, he drank in the feel of the Quarter, letting it seep into him and exciting him.

"Mama, look at me. I did this for you," Sasa pleaded. Reaching out, her mother's hand slipped out of her grip.

Sandra Lambert stood with her back to her daughter, shutting her out. But Sasa was thankful to see she was strong enough to stand on her own two feet and stubbornly refuse to do anything.

"Please, Mama. I couldn't bear to see you suffer anymore. Look at how much you've improved. I'd rather deal with you fighting with me any day over watching you waste away in agony in that bed."

Slowly her mother turned to face her, and Sasa saw for the first time how much she'd truly changed. Her tired face she'd seen for so long looked firm and rejuvenated. The wrinkles had disappeared. And her body, which she'd seen lying in a bed for years, looked healthy and strong, her clothes no longer hanging off a skeletal frame.

"What have you done to me, Sasa?"

"You look wonderful—like the woman you were before Papa left. You won't have to suffer anymore. I promise. Everything will be fine. You'll see."

Her mother lifted her hand in front of her face and stared at it. "Look."

Sasa couldn't deny her mother looked much paler than she had before Tatiana had sired her. It was a small price to pay for the end of her suffering, though. Taking her hand in hers, Sasa brought it to her mouth and pressed her lips in a kiss against the cool skin. She looked up into the alert brown eyes that stared down at her full of emotion.

"Mama, you're out of that terrible bed and strong enough to argue with me. I never thought I'd see you like this again. I know you may be angry with me now, but you'll see. Things will be better for us from now on."

Her mother tore her hand from Sasa's grip. "How can you say that? I'm a monster!"

The horror on her mother's face nearly broke Sasa's heart. "Don't say that, Mama! You're the same person you've always been. Just better."

Sasa watched in sadness as her mother sunk into the loveseat next to her. "I'm a monster who drinks blood, baby," she said quietly into her hands covering her face as she began to sob.

Dropping to her knees beside her, Sasa wanted to cry too. Like she used to when she was a child, she laid her head against her mother's leg and closed her eyes.

"Mama, you're not a monster. Vampires aren't monsters. They eat and drink just like us—well, except for the blood. But that can be controlled. I know this for a fact. All you have to do is drink the blood I left for you, and everything will be okay."

Her mother began to tenderly stroke her hair, and Sasa breathed a sigh of relief. Just as when she was a young girl, her mother could make her feel better just with the touch of her hand.

"Oh, baby, I know you meant well, but..." Sandra Lambert's speech broke off as she began to cry.

Sasa looked up and watched her mother's sad expression. "Please don't cry. I promise it'll be okay. Just don't worry. Let's just be happy you're better."

Nodding, her mother stroked her cheek. "Sasa, what if I...want to..."

"No, it doesn't work like that, Mama. I was with one last night and nothing like that happened with him."

Sasa saw the look of shock on her mother's face and sheepishly said, "You said I should go out and make some new friends."

Her mother's expression turned deathly serious. "Sasa, what have you gotten into? Vampires aren't to be trifled with. The one you had do this to me looked like a barracuda. You're looking to get hurt, baby."

Sasa rose to her feet and leaned down to kiss her mother's forehead. "Trust me, Mama. I know what I'm doing."

Quietly, her mother said, "I hope so baby."

Sasa hoped so too. Her time with Vasilije had shown her an entirely different side of vampires from the one she'd seen from Tatiana, but she had to remember they could be killers as easily as lovers.

The memory of making love with him the night before made her blush, and Sasa quickly sat down next to her mother and hugged her, hiding her face in the crook of her neck. In her mother's arms, she felt safe. Closing her eyes, she let her mind drift back to Vasilije.

"Mama, what kind of name is Sasa?"

Sandra Lambert gently squeezed her daughter's shoulders. "It was a name from your papa's side."

"I know, but what kind of name is it?"

"It's Cherokee. Your papa's granddaddy was a Cherokee. It's where you got your beautiful hair from."

"What's it mean?"

Her mother lifted Sasa's chin and smiled down at her. "I don't know. All I know is that from that first moment I saw you in my arms, I knew no other name would fit. You were my Sasa."

"I'll always be your Sasa, Mama. Always."

As she repeated always, the truth of what she'd done fully dawned on her. Always had an entirely different meaning now.

VASILIJE LOOKED around the crowded bar, his gaze sharp with need. As much as he knew he should be hunting for Teagan's killer, for the second night in a row, desire won out over vengeance. Breathing deeply, the thick smoky air filled his lungs and nearly sickened him. He couldn't remember when he'd last fed, and hunger pinched at him as he mentally rejected one person after another in front of him.

Even he had no idea why he insisted on being so fucking picky. What did it matter what his target looked like? One was the same as the next, and they all had what he wanted. Since he couldn't feed from one of his vampires, whichever one of the humans around him would do.

But that's not who he was.

He found a seat in a corner, away from the crowd pushing their way toward the bar, and surveyed his choices. In frustration, he wondered why every bar on every continent seemed to come equipped with the same cast of characters. Innocent, doe-eyed blond in a barely there dress. Exotic looking brunette who looked like she was dying to get fucked. Twenty-something males who all looked like stupid frat boys. The first two bored him, and the third disgusted him and reminded him of Alex.

Whatever he thought of his choices, he had to feed soon. He couldn't go much longer if he wanted to have the strength to find the fuck who'd staked Teagan. Another sweep of the crowd brought him to someone who'd do. Covered in alcohol from the woman who'd just stormed away from him, he'd be easy to persuade that leaving was a good idea.

In the blink of an eye, Vasilije was next to him. "I'm sure she'll be back."

The man gave a fake smile as he wiped gin and tonic from his face. "Doesn't matter. We were over anyway."

Even better.

"Sure. And in this crowd, how hard can it be to replace her?"

The man turned to look at Vasilije for the first time and smiled. "Yeah, you got that right. I can find another piece of ass here if I wanted to, but fuck 'em, right?"

Focusing his eyes on the man's, Vasilije began to speak slowly and methodically to the person who would provide him what he needed. "What's your name?"

The man responded to the low tone of Vasilije's voice already beginning to hypnotize him. "Jeremy. Jeremy Canter."

Never averting his gaze, Vasilije answered, "Well, Jeremy Canter, how would you like to leave here and find a good time somewhere else?"

"Okay."

"Listen carefully to me, Jeremy. You're going to follow me."

Nodding, Jeremy replied, his voice flat and monotone, "Yes, I'll follow you."

Vasilije leaned in and whispered a short chant to ensure Jeremy's willing compliance before turning toward the door. His new friend dutifully followed behind, deeply hypnotized and under the vampire's complete control.

As they left the bar, Vasilije scanned the neighborhood nearby for somewhere secluded. A park would have been nice, but all he saw were more bars and restaurants. Turning to Jeremy, he asked, "Do you live near here?"

The man shook his head. "Ruston."

Unsure if that was a street name or a city, Vasilije began making his way through the crowds of the Quarter. A dark alley would have to do. Spying one, he led Jeremy through the bustling drunken mob. A left off Royal and he'd found the perfect spot to feed.

As his eyes adjusted to the sudden darkness, he saw they were alone, except for a few well-fed rats that scurried away as they moved toward them. Vasilije maneuvered around a pile of boxes thrown out for garbage and finding an empty spot along the brick walls lining the alley, took hold of Jeremy.

"Just relax," he whispered next to his ear in the same hypnotic tone as before. "And stay still."

Vasilije's mouth touched the soft skin of Jeremy's neck just over his slowly throbbing pulse. Fangs punched into his mouth as Vasilije prepared for the first blood he'd had in days. Jeremy instinctively flinched, and Vasilije steadied his head with a hand on his jaw. "Still," he ordered sharply and then a second later he sunk his teeth into the man's vein.

The thick liquid he hungered for slowly slid past his lips and over his tongue, its taste the usual tanginess. As Jeremy's blood began to flow down his throat, Vasilije closed his eyes and pretended the man was one of his own, a fantasy he sometimes found necessary to enjoy the blood of a human.

Jeremy made soft, pleading noises at first but then fell silent, his hypnotic state overpowering his body's natural reaction to attack. Vasilije was thankful he gave in easily as he had no desire to fight for this tonight.

As the blood continued to drain down his throat, Vasilije's mind traveled back to thoughts of Sasa. He hadn't seen or heard from her since they'd drifted off to sleep in one another's arms the day before, but she'd crossed his mind a few times since then. Some small part of him felt like prick that he'd slept with her. She was Teagan's girlfriend, for fuck's sake.

Teagan.

Just the thought of him still stabbed at Vasilije's gut. Teagan gone from the Earth wasn't something he wanted to accept. Rage exploded in his mind at the thought of the stake plunging into Teagan's heart and the look of surprise that surely crossed his face just before his body turned to dust.

Vasilije's mouth pulled roughly at Jeremy's neck as the feeling of loss overwhelmed more pleasurable emotions. Without knowing, he took him past the point of no return. Lifting his head, he looked into Jeremy's eyes all glazed over and knew he had a decision to make. Either he drained him and left him to die, or he turned him and made him one of his own.

Wiping the blood from the corners of his mouth, he

looked at Jeremy's face for a moment, studying him. The similarity to Teagan struck him as his gaze glided over his light brown hair, brown eyes, and slightly crooked nose.

Instinct took over and his fangs sunk into his own wrist to begin the process of making Jeremy a vampire. Close to death, Jeremy's pale face turned toward him, his empty eyes staring up at him. For a second, Vasilije felt a pang of guilt. Alex he'd wanted, but Jeremy was a mistake a four-hundred-year-old vampire knew better than to make.

Pressing his wrist to Jeremy's mouth, Vasilije forced him to drink and as he began to greedily take what he needed, Vasilije closed his eyes, letting the feeling of siring another vampire take him over.

7

Vasilije awoke from a long day's rest almost as tired as when he'd finally gotten to bed just before dawn. Jeremy had needed the attention required of a sire and struggled in his first hours as a vampire. After resisting for almost two hours and refusing to accept his new life, he finally succumbed to the power of an ancient spell Vasilije reluctantly used on him. Its effect would last for at least another day and keep the new vampire sedated, which would give Vasilije time to begin his search for Teagan's killer.

Throwing his arm over his eyes, Vasilije considered his choices, mainly where he'd find his own kind. A Mecca of sorts for vampires, New Orleans provided him with ample opportunities to meet with others like him. The problem wasn't where to find them but which place to begin.

As he lay there in thought, his sharp sense of hearing picked up the sound of the doorknob slowly turning on the front door. Quickly, he leapt out of bed and positioned himself behind the bedroom door. In moments, the uninvited guest stepped into the room and he had them pushed up against the wall, under his control.

One look at the person in front of him told Vasilije he was in no danger.

"Sasa, pet, you're going to get yourself hurt doing things like that. You're lucky I didn't snap your neck."

Undeterred by his greeting, Sasa said, "Who's the guy on the couch? I didn't know you knew anyone here but me."

Backing away from her, a still naked Vasilije walked casually over to where his clothes were flung over the back of a chair. As he stepped into his pants, he said, "And Teagan. But that's a new friend. Jeremy."

Sasa walked across the room and stopped in front of him, her hands on her hips. "When you say friend, do you mean a drinking buddy? Maybe a guy you plan to watch the game with tonight?"

Her questions amused him. "Do I look like someone who watches games?"

"Well, no. Then who is he?"

Vasilije slipped his shirt on, leaving it unbuttoned. "He's a vampire, Sasa." To punctuate his point, he smiled and let his fangs click into his mouth. "Remember, vampire?"

Sasa stepped back with a look of surprise on her face. "Did you make him into a vampire? Why?"

Vasilije stopped and thought about what a ludicrous question that was. Why did he sire a vampire? That was like asking humans why they breathed or why they ate.

"I'm a vampire, love. It's what we do."

Walking past her, he looked for where he'd left his

shoes hours before. As he finished dressing, she grabbed his arm and he turned to see her disturbed expression.

"You didn't do that to me. You didn't even bite me."

"Regretting that?" he teased.

"I'm serious. How can you say that's what you do since you didn't do that to me?"

"Sasa, you were Teagan's girlfriend. You're obviously someone my kind accepts, so I respected your choice."

The look on her face seemed to indicate she was hurt. Confused, he considered asking what was wrong but assumed it wouldn't take long before he found out what was bothering her. He wasn't wrong.

"You don't have to go around biting people, do you? And...well...would you if I hadn't asked you not to?"

Vasilije ran his finger down the side of her face and then down her neck, letting his gaze follow its trail. Even frustrated like she was, she still stirred something in him that made him want her. Looking up into her eyes, he licked his lips at the thought of just a taste of the woman standing so close to him and smiled.

"No to the first question. And as for the second question, with pleasure."

An awkward silence hung in the air and Vasilije wondered if he'd ever have the chance to have her that way. He would have already, if she hadn't asked him not to. Whether he should have slept with her was a question to be debated, but drinking from her was something he was sure Teagan would have allowed, even encouraged, knowing his past times with him.

"Sasa, I have to go. I have work to do."

Tagging along behind him, she said, "Great. I'm coming with you."

Vasilije stopped dead and spun around. "No. You don't want to go where I'm going."

Putting her hands back on her hips, she frowned. "I thought we got this bullshit out of the way. I want to help you find Teagan's killer."

"I'm going to see others like me. You seem to have developed a problem with vampires."

Sasa followed Vasilije's gaze toward a sleeping Jeremy on the couch. "I'm going. I'm not worried. You protected me the other night at the bar, so I trust you."

Vasilije looked at her defiant expression and wondered how she'd safely made it this far in life. Trusting a vampire she barely knew was dangerous. How naive she was.

"I protected you from a bar full of horny men who wanted to get their dicks wet. A room full of vampires might be a different story."

"Will they be horny too?" she asked sarcastically.

Shaking his head, Vasilije had to smile. "That mouth is going to get you in trouble, pet. If I let you come with me, you have to promise you'll keep it shut."

Reluctantly, Sasa agreed. "Fine. But do you really think I might be in danger where we're going?"

"Don't worry. Just act like you're mine and you'll be fine."

"Your what?"

"Mine. Act like you're my girlfriend, lover, whatever you want to call it and you'll be fine. A vampire wouldn't mess with another vampire's woman without his permission."

As they headed out the door, Vasilije cringed at the irony of what he'd just said. They walked silently through the night, and when they arrived at a large house that looked like every Southern house he'd ever seen in the movies, he hoped he hadn't made a mistake allowing her to join him in the New Orleans vampire scene.

"What is this place, Vasilije?" Sasa asked as she looked at the home in front of her.

"The offices of the Louisiana Archon."

As he stepped past her, Sasa grabbed his hand to stop him. "What's a vampire archon?"

Suddenly a chill ran across her skin. She'd expected they'd meet some of his fellow vampires at a bar or some other public place. Somewhere out in the open where she'd be safe. Not some out of the way house of some powerful vampire with a title.

"Don't worry. This is just a formality. As a foreigner, I have to inform the local officials of my whereabouts in their area."

"Oh, like a sex offender?"

Sasa immediately saw that Vasilije hadn't appreciated her joke.

"Love, what did I tell you about your mouth? No one will ever believe you're mine if you say things like that. No self-respecting vampire male would have a female who talked to him like that." As he began climbing the steps to the front door, she heard him mumble, "Nor do I suspect a human male."

Sasa stood in stunned silence as he continued up the stairs. Her mouth was not the reason she was alone! She had her mother to take care of—or she had. Plus she had to find work to put food on the table and keep a roof over their heads. And then there was the reality of the dating scene. No, there were many reasons why she was still single.

Indignant at his insult, she snapped, "I'll have you know there are many men who would love to call themselves mine!"

Vasilije turned around and with a smile that sent a jolt of pleasure straight to between her legs said, "I have no doubt, love. Could we discuss your appeal later after we finish here? I promise to give you my undivided attention."

God, he was infuriating! Just when she wanted to be angry with him, he turned on the charm like he was turning on a light and she wanted to melt.

This is what I get for having sex with him.

Sasa grudgingly stomped up the stairs to join him and stood scowling at the door.

"You're going to have to pretend you like me a bit more than that, Sasa."

Unable to stop herself, she grimaced and shot back, "Don't worry about me. I can be quite an actress when I need to be."

"Good. Now take my hand and don't let go."

Placing her hand in his, she was once again surprised to feel her body respond to him. Curious, and a little insecure, she wondered if he felt anything for her. Focusing on his emotions, she waited to feel any sense of attraction from him. As he rang the doorbell and waited for an answer, all she felt coming from him was irritation and a tiny flash of fear.

Nothing else. No desire for her at all.

The front door opened and someone she assumed was a butler listened as Vasilije explained the reason for his visit. Sasa barely listened, consumed instead by the fact that he seemed to feel nothing in response to her being so close.

She wasn't sure why she felt anything for him. He should only be the vampire she was spying on for Tatiana. That's all he was supposed to be. Instead, she found herself thinking about him when she wasn't around him, remembering how he felt next to her, inside her.

Vasilije turned to look at her and nodded his head toward the man they had to follow inside. Sasa dutifully walked next to him while she considered her dilemma.

Definitely some kind of spell or something. Look at those eyes. Ice blue and just as cold looking. And that hair. Jet black. Definitely not the brown or blond I prefer. And that mouth? Hello? He's got fangs, for God's sake! No, it must be some vampire trick he's used on me.

He roused her from her daydreaming with a nudge of his knee against her leg, and Sasa looked down where their bodies touched, avoiding his gaze. "What?"

"You faded out on me for a bit. Are you okay? You don't need to be afraid. I won't let anyone harm you."

"I'm fine. What's going on?"

"We're waiting for the Archon. Once I finish this legal formality, then we'll begin hunting for Teagan's killer."

Vasilije squeezed her hand as he said Teagan's name, as if in sympathy for her loss. Sasa saw the same look of sadness she'd seen that first night cross his face for just a moment and then it was gone.

The mention of Teagan's name brought her situation

back into sharp focus. She was working for Tatiana against Vasilije, and if she didn't begin to remember that, she was going to have much bigger problems that him not wanting her.

Just then a man Sasa instantly understood she should fear entered the room. Rather ordinary in appearance, he was much shorter than Vasilije's just over six foot frame and looked like someone who would easily blend into a crowd. But it wasn't his looks that made Sasa uneasy. As soon as he'd come near her, she'd felt a coldness—almost like an evil presence. As he sat down in front of them, it took everything in her not to run away. Squeezing Vasilije's hand, she hoped if the man attempted to harm her Vasilije could protect her, like he'd promised.

"What can I do for you?"

"Just following the law. I plan to be in New Orleans for a while. Personal business."

"Here to see one of your vampires? Have you registered with my office?"

"I plan to."

"And her?"

Scared stiff, Sasa nervously thought to herself that she might explode with laughter if he told the Archon that he planned to be in her for a while too.

"She's part of that personal business."

The Archon's face remained emotionless, except for a tiny smile that showed just the tips of his fangs. Slowly, almost seductively, he ran his tongue across his top teeth as he moved his gaze from Vasilije to her.

Staring as her like she was an entree on some living menu, he continued to address Vasilije. "I don't know what is customary where you come from, but here in

New Orleans, we don't generally have humans on our arms. Unless she's a slave."

Vasilije gently squeezed her hand as he answered. "She's mine. What I do with her is my business."

The Archon slowly turned his eyes back to Vasilije and then in a hollow voice said, "Enjoy your time in my area. Remember, however, you're not in London. We're a bit more close-knit here."

With that, he rose from behind his desk and stiffly walked out of the room, offering Vasilije no handshake or even a polite goodbye.

"It's time to go, Sasa."

Vasilije led the way back outside, saying nothing until the two of them were almost a block away. Unlike just a few minutes earlier, Sasa felt waves of emotion coming from him now.

"It's best if you go home now, love."

Sasa couldn't believe she was going to have to deal with this again. "Vasilije, no. Why do you keep pushing me away from helping you? I'm staying."

His response surprised her. Blue eyes wide with emotion stared down at her. "I can't promise I can protect you, Sasa. Please go home. I don't want to see you hurt."

"You're just scaring me, so I'll leave."

Suddenly, he grabbed her upper arms, as if to shake her. Fear of him raced through her for the first time.

"Sasa, you need to be scared. Didn't you hear how the Archon spoke to me? And didn't you listen when he basically said you should be a slave?"

"Well, he wasn't very nice, but not every vampire can be you."

Vasilije dropped his hands, obviously frustrated, and

looked up toward the night sky. Maybe her joking had gone too far.

"You're not kidding, are you?"

Lowering his gaze to meet hers, his blue eyes showed concern more than anything else. "Sasa, something is very wrong. That man knew everything about me. I never mentioned where I'm from and that one of my vampires lived here, and my accent isn't English, yet he referred to me being from London and knows about Teagan."

"What are you saying?"

Shaking his head, he took her hand and began walking. "I don't know. Something doesn't feel right. And that part about humans as slaves? That's not an opinion that's generally held by the Archons."

"How would he know who you are? Did you mention anything to anyone?"

"No. The only people I've spoken to since I've gotten here are you and Jeremy. I've done some nosing around to find where the local groups are who might know something about Teagan's murder, but I haven't said a thing to anyone."

Sasa turned to look away, afraid what she was thinking was written all over her face. There was someone else in New Orleans who knew where he was from. Had she contacted the Archon? If so, why since she was in town expressly to get revenge on Vasilije?

Turning back, she asked, "And did he really mean I should be a slave?"

"Not the kind you think. He meant a bleeder."

Sasa felt her own blood run cold. "Bleeder? What's that?"

Vasilije pulled her up next to him. "Sasa, it's exactly

what it says. As my bleeder, you'd be mine to feed on whenever I chose. Vampires prefer to feed from their own, but some think it's acceptable to keep a human for times when there isn't one of us around."

"I'm confused. Why wouldn't you just sire a vampire instead of making a human a slave?"

"I would, but some of my kind want to punish humans for hunting us."

Sasa felt sick to her stomach. "Vasilije, maybe I won't go with you."

Bending down, he placed a soft kiss on her forehead. "Good. I'd feel much better if you were safe at home."

"Okay. I'll go."

"Go home and stay there, Sasa. I'll contact you later."

Sasa left Vasilije a few blocks from her house, but as she walked home, she dreaded staying in that house alone. It seemed so empty now that her mother was gone, and what had always felt welcoming and secure now felt hollow and lonely. Hopping on the streetcar, she made her way to Teagan's house in the Garden District and found Jeremy still fast asleep on the couch.

As she crawled into the bed she and Vasilije had shared, a calmness enveloped her. Breathing deeply, she let Vasilije's sweetly musky scent fill her nose. Uniquely him, it made her feel safe.

Drifting off to sleep, she tried to push the memory of what the Archon had said out of her mind. Maybe what her mother had said was true. Maybe vampires were monsters.

Well, maybe not all of them.

"YOUR MAN JUST LEFT. To say I was surprised when he was announced would be an understatement. All I want to know is why isn't he dead yet?"

Tatiana sat listening to the Louisiana Archon chastise her, more interested in how Vasilije had acted toward Sasa than anything else. "I want to have my revenge on him first."

Steel gray eyes shot back a look of irritation at her. "You have a job to do for us, Tatiana. That job doesn't include revenge for whatever slight this vampire has inflicted on you."

"It's far more than a slight, your honor. I told you I made a formal complaint about him in London. Vampire law says..."

The Archon cut her off with an angry wave of his hand. "I know what you charged in London, and we found that his infraction wasn't serious enough for us to get involved in a formal hearing. Find another boy to play with. But not before you do what you've been instructed. We chose you because you claim to hate him. Were we wrong?"

The hate she felt for Vasilije made her fingers numb it was so strong. "No, you weren't wrong. I just want to make him suffer before I kill him."

The Archon stood from behind his desk and walked to where she sat. Looking down at her, he straightened his tie and adjusted his suit coat before he spoke. "He'll suffer when you kill him. You may take as long to do the actual deed as you like, but no more of this playing around. We don't much care one way or another what happens to the girl, but if you're going to kill her too, make sure it's clean and not something I have to deal with afterward. Do you understand me?"

"Yes, sir."

As the Archon walked out of his office, Tatiana sat alone silently cursing the laws of their world. Vasilije had broken their rules, no matter what the Archons said, and he needed to pay for that. Whatever bigger plan they had didn't mean anything compared to her need for revenge. Alex was the last straw, and this time, Vasilije wasn't going to get away with what he'd done.

8

It was almost three a.m. by the time Vasilije got back to Teagan's, and all he wanted was the feel of his mattress against his back and the chance to stretch out his tired legs. He'd learned very little about who could be behind Teagan's murder. The group of vampires he'd visited in the Quarter seemed to believe some hunters in the area could be responsible, but he remained unconvinced.

At least they'd spoken to him. The vampires outside the city—Swamprats, as the Quarter group called them—were so paranoid of outsiders they wouldn't even listen to his questions. After dealing with both groups, all he knew was the New Orleans vampires were an entirely different breed than what he was used to.

Teagan, how the fuck did you deal with them?

As he passed by Jeremy on the couch, he saw him begin to stir as the spell's effect began to wear off. Hopefully, he still had a few hours before he woke up and he had to deal with him.

Fuck. And they call this place The Big Easy?

In the dark, he stripped out of his clothes and headed for the bed. Even before he made it there, he saw her sleeping. She looked like an angel, her hands folded under her cheek on the pillow next to his.

What is she doing here?

As quietly as he could, he slid under the covers, careful not to wake her. Slowly, his body melded into the comfort of the bed beneath him, and the night's events faded into the back of his mind.

He turned to look to his left as Sasa sighed in her sleep. She looked so comfortable, so right next to him. Had she always slept on that side next to Teagan?

Vasilije caught himself as he began to imagine them together in the very bed he now shared with her. Jealousy stung him at the thought of Teagan touching her. Making love to her. Had he loved her? Had she loved him?

Teagan had never been a man to devote himself to one woman, so Vasilije doubted it had been love on his side. Strangely, that didn't give him any comfort. The idea that Sasa had given her heart to someone who didn't love her in return gnawed at him.

Turning the light on, she asked, "Did you find anything out?"

The sound of her voice roused him from his thoughts. As he considered her question, she propped her head up on her hand and looked up at him, waiting for an answer.

"What are you doing here, Sasa?"

"I asked first."

"Not much."

Sasa made a noise to show her sympathy and lowered her head to the pillow. The way she looked at him, like he imagined a wife did at a husband, made him want to set things straight.

"Why are you here?"

For a long moment, she was silent. Then in a voice that threatened to undo his resolve, she said, "I didn't want to be alone."

Jesus, how can anyone be so open?

"Sasa, I can't replace Teagan. I'm not like him."

She closed her eyes and silently lay next to him, but he had to continue.

"I can't be what he was."

Sasa looked up at him with hurt in her eyes. "Don't...don't say that."

"I'm not a boyfriend. I'm a man who fucks the girl-friend of his dead friend."

The words rang in his ears, sounding far harsher than he intended them to be. Instinctively, he turned his face away from her, unable to deal with the sadness he was sure he'd see.

Sasa gently touched his stomach, exciting him more than he wished.

"Look at me. Please."

Vasilije looked back at her and cringed at the pain he saw on her face. "Sasa...don't."

"Don't talk like that about what we've done together."

"This is nothing. This is two people consoling them-selves. That's all."

Fuck. He knew he was being an asshole, but whatever she was feeling—whatever she thought they were—couldn't be.

As he saw her face register the hurt from his words, he sensed the bedroom door open. Before he could intercept Jeremy, he was at his side of the bed, a new vampire hungry for blood.

"Whatever you did to make me pass out only made me hungry. Feed me."

Jeremy was as obnoxious as he'd been before the spell, but since Vasilije had created this mess, he knew he had to deal with it. Nature took over and his fangs punched down into his mouth. Pressing against his wrist, he pierced his own skin and opened a vein. Blood oozed down his inner arm as he lifted his wrist to Jeremy's mouth.

"Drink."

Doing as he was ordered, Jeremy's mouth drew eagerly on Vasilije's wrist, silencing him for at least a short time. Sasa lay staring up at the scene, her eyes wide with curiosity.

"This is what I am, Sasa. Not a boyfriend. Not some roommate. Vampire."

She said nothing and seemed intently interested in Jeremy's feeding. Her eyes were riveted to his wrist, where Jeremy continued to greedily lap up the blood his body craved. Vasilije wanted her to watch. She needed to see exactly what he was so whatever fantasy she'd created disappeared quickly.

Sasa stopped watching and left the bed. Standing there in just her panties and one of Teagan's t-shirts, she looked so innocent—far too innocent to be involved with him. He waited for her to say something. Anything. Goodbye. Tell him he could go fuck himself. But she just silently stood while Jeremy finished.

Vasilije yanked his wrist away from Jeremy's mouth and slid his tongue over the wound to seal it. Eyes closed, he allowed himself to enjoy the feelings feeding one of his vampires brought out in him. He'd deal with Sasa in a minute, but for now, he let the joy ease into him.

Sasa made a noise as she rounded the corner of the bed, and Vasilije slowly opened his eyes to see her approaching his side of the bed. Before he could say a word, she had Jeremy pushed against the wall. His newest vampire wasted little time responding to her, the question of her relationship with his sire obviously of little consequence to him.

Vasilije sat stunned as he watched them move from mere kissing to something far more erotic. Sasa stood on her toes to wrap her arms around Jeremy's neck, causing her shirt to rise just above the bottom of her pretty ass. Jeremy's hand slid down to cup that ass before he pulled her into his body. Young and eager, he slid his fingers under her panties, grazing the delicate skin Vasilije had known just days before.

Vasilije knew what she was doing. A little ploy to make him jealous. And it was working.

Fuck her. He wasn't some local yokel frat boy like Jeremy. He was a four-hundred-year-old vampire. He could have any woman he wanted. If she wanted some boy barely out of adolescence, she could have him.

But he wasn't going to sit idly by and watch.

One swift movement brought him directly behind Sasa, his erect cock pressing against her back. His voice low and deep, he spoke quietly as he began to hypnotize her. "You want this, Sasa. Let your body be ours. Let go."

Vasilije ran his hands over her taut belly and dainty little panties wet from desire for what his words promised. As Jeremy continued his focus on her mouth,

Vasilije paid attention to other regions of her body he already knew intimately. Crouching, he slid those drenched panties down her beautiful legs and off her feet, tossing them aside dismissively.

Sasa obeyed his command and arched to accommodate his sensual caresses as his fingers trailed from her swollen clit to her opening. Each pass through her soft folds elicited needy moans from her, exciting him more.

He planted small kisses along her hip as he played with her cunt, knowing she wanted so much more than kisses and teasing. Above, Jeremy fondled her excited nipples, and Sasa pushed her ass out to encourage Vasilije to finally do more than play with her.

Standing to his full height, he pushed his stiff cock between her legs, just grazing where he knew she so desperately wanted him to stay. She moaned into Jeremy's mouth, a begging mew that sent a jolt of arousal from Vasilije's balls through his erection. From this angle, he was at a distinct disadvantage, though. That had to change.

"Jeremy, behind her," he ordered as he moved to slide in front of her.

As the younger vampire took his position at her back, Vasilije brought her up against his body. "Focus on her legs."

Sasa wrapped her arms around his neck and her mouth rooted for his. So willing, she rolled her hips against him, leaving evidence of her desire on his stiff cock. This was going to be quite enjoyable.

Jeremy dropped to his knees and began kissing her thighs. Now in the position of power, Vasilije took control of Sasa, kissing her deeply as she moaned into his mouth.

He liked the thought of turning the tables on her little game.

Little girls shouldn't play with fire.

He spoke to her, his voice the same hypnotic tone as before as he slowly stroked her neck and stared into her eyes. "Sasa, look at me. You will do whatever I tell you to. Do you understand?"

Sasa smiled and nodded. "Yes, Vasilije."

"Tell me what you want, love."

She was silent for a moment and then quietly she said next to his ear, "I want you to stop trying to hypnotize me. It won't work. And since I mean nothing to you, I want him, not you. So why don't you go back to watching?"

Sasa stared defiantly up at him, her face the picture of smugness. So, she wanted to test him? Fine. Now she'd see what she got when she played games with a vampire.

In the low, deep voice of a sire, he commanded, "Jeremy, go back to the couch. Now."

Jeremy immediately rose to his feet and skulked away, unable to disobey his sire's command. As he closed the door behind him, Vasilije roughly pulled Sasa to meet his body.

"Mine."

Sasa worked to wriggle out of his hold as she protested his claim. "I'm nothing to you. Let me go!"

Her words—his words—enraged him. She wasn't nothing to him. At that moment, she was the only thing that mattered in the world. The feel of her pressed against him as he held her tightly to his body made his claim all the more real.

Mine.

Vasilije spun them around and pinned her against the

wall. One hand captured her hands above her head, and the other cupped her sex and pressed against her tightened bud.

Sasa looked up at him, her eyes wide with surprise as she seemed to realize what she'd awakened in him. "Vasilije, please..."

He slid a finger through her wet slit, gliding up and down with her moans. Her eyes closed, and she arched toward his body, needy for his touch. Vasilije leaned close to her ear, and groaning at his own need to be inside her, whispered, "Tell me you don't want this and I'll release you. If not, you're mine."

He didn't have to wait for her answer. Her mouth was on his neck, kissing him as she worked to tip her hips to make her pussy more available to him. When she spoke, her voice was edged with desire, like music to his ears.

"Make me yours."

Her words sent his body into overdrive, and he released her hands to lift her off the ground. She clung to him as she pleaded for him to hurry. God, he wanted to be inside her!

Sasa wrapped her legs around his waist and slid up and down against his cock, coating him in her slickness. His stomach muscles tightened at each pass over the length of him, and need pressed on him more than ever now.

Quickly, he turned back toward the bed and let her pull him down with her. Catching himself with his hands, he stopped for a moment as he hovered over her. She looked so beautiful, her warm brown hair fanned out behind her and falling onto the t-shirt she still wore.

Teagan's t-shirt.

Jealously spiked in Vasilije and his hands twitched with the need to rip the shirt from her body. "Take the shirt off," he growled possessively.

Sasa did as he ordered and reached out to touch him. "Hurry, please..."

The sound of her voice so full of need cut through him, and he wasted no more time. Pushing her knees apart, he plunged into her until he was fully nested deep inside her. For just a moment, he stilled, reveling in the feeling of her tight cunt surrounding him.

Wanting more, she gently began bucking against him. "Vasilije, don't tease me," she pleaded.

"Be careful what you ask for, pet," he said in her ear as he began thrusting his hips forward and back, filling her then retreating over and over. Her body closed in around him each time he left her, only to open to welcome him each time he returned.

Sasa rolled him onto his back and began to ride him. Vasilije watched in wonder at the woman who'd looked so innocent just a few minutes earlier now rode his cock. Before he took back control, he wanted to watch her beautiful face as he made her come. Slowly, he drew circles on her tight bud with the pad of his thumb as she inched closer to surrender. Her eyes closed, and her mouth opened slightly as she began to pant in time with his movements. Almost imperceptibly, her body tightened around his cock, milking it with spasms that rapidly swept over her entire body. "Yes! Don't stop...yes..."

She threw her head back in ecstasy, becoming even more beautiful in her climax. Vasilije watched with pleasure knowing he'd given her that. Not Jeremy. Not any other man. Him. When she'd recovered from the shocks wracking her body, she leaned down and kissed him tenderly on the cheek. Out of breath, she panted, "That was incredible."

Stroking her back, he smiled. It had been incredible, and he hadn't even come.

"Your turn."

Vasilije's attention focused on where Sasa's mouth traveled over his chest. He watched as she ran her tongue over his nipple before taking it into her mouth to gently suck it between her lips. Almost tentatively, she bit down, and waves of pleasure raced through his body.

While she thrilled him with her mouth, her hand slid lower to palm his still hard cock. Wrapping her fingers around him, she leisurely stroked down to the base and back up to the tip again. She knew exactly how to excite him.

Vasilije let the sensations roll over him and hissed his approval. "Faster."

She obeyed, and as her hand slid over his skin, her eyes seemed to dance as her gaze met his. Lifting her head, she moved up to kiss him deeply. But that wasn't enough. He wanted more. Much more.

Grabbing her hair, he tugged her head back. "I want more than your hand, love. Sit back on me."

Sasa flung her leg over his body and positioned herself over him as Vasilije sat up to face her. "Wrap your legs around me, Sasa. I want to be as deep as I can inside you."

He saw the look of hesitation come over her. Reluctantly, she moved to do as he'd said, whispering, "I've never..."

"Don't worry. You'll love it."

He slid into her completely and felt her skin touch his as their hips met one another. It was as if she were made to fit him, her body a perfect match for his.

"How are we supposed to move?" she asked innocently. "I'm on top, but I have no leverage."

Vasilije couldn't help but smile. Even with him buried balls deep in her, she was that same curious soul who'd charmed him from their first meeting. "Shhhh, just look into my eyes and let yourself go."

Her deep brown eyes focused on his, and he spoke to her softly, hoping not to scare her. "Tell me you want to be mine, Sasa. I want to hear the words come from your mouth."

He waited as she stayed silent, but her gaze never wavered. Was she thinking of saying yes, or was she deciding how to refuse knowing she was as close to him as any woman could be? Her eyes betrayed nothing of what was going on behind them.

"Sasa?"

Gently, she pushed the strands of hair that hung near his face as her gaze traveled to his mouth. With one finger, she stroked the seam of his lips, dipping in cautiously when she felt his fangs. Staring at them, she asked, "Will it hurt?"

Silently, he shook his head knowing he was lying. It would hurt for a moment at first, but then the pleasure would overwhelm the pain.

"I need to know this is more than nothing to you."

The vulnerability in her voice sliced through him, and he regretted every word he'd said earlier. Those had been the words of denial by a man who didn't want to admit he truly enjoyed being around her, naked or not.

The words of a man who'd been alone so long that he thought it was all right.

Vasilije let his hands glide over the silky skin of her back and up to cradle her face. His thumbs stroked next to the corners of her mouth, and she smiled as she waited for his answer.

"You mean far more than nothing to me, love. I was just being a fool when I said this was nothing."

His words made her eyes soften and she whispered, "Yes" so quietly he wasn't sure he'd heard her correctly. Sasa turned her head and pulled back her hair, exposing her neck.

She'd said yes.

Vasilije's fangs grew to their full length as the gentle pulse in her neck pounded softly against her skin. For a moment, he stared in sweet anticipation of how it would feel as he sunk into her. How she would taste on his tongue. Only the sting of his fangs cutting into his lower lip brought him back to reality.

"Hold on to me. And when your orgasm begins, just let it take you over. I don't want to hurt you if you begin thrashing around."

"Oh."

He heard the fear come into her voice and tried to calm her. "I promise you'll love it."

The truth was he was worried she might love it too much. Even worse, since she obviously couldn't be hypnotized—why was that? He'd definitely have to figure that out—he wouldn't be able to make her forget about drinking from her. If she became too attached...

He didn't want to think about that now. Now all he

wanted was the pure pleasure that came from drinking a woman's blood while he was deep inside her.

The pleasure of tasting this woman for the first time.

His lips lightly grazed over her skin before he paused where he'd sink his fangs into her. He inhaled the sweet scent of her skin as he opened his lips, and pressing against her delicate skin, his teeth pierced it and the vein below. Her warm blood slowly seeped into his mouth, making his cock harden like iron.

Sasa was his.

9

At the first touch of Vasilije's fangs, Sasa jumped, but now as he sank into her skin, pain unlike any she'd ever felt bolted through her. He'd lied! This hurt like hell!

She opened her mouth to cry out, but just then the pain turned to a sweet ache that reached to every cell in her body, nearly taking her breath away. For a moment, he eased his drinking, making the feeling subside. Desperate to feel it again, she held his head to her, urging him to continue.

"Don't stop," she begged breathlessly.

Vasilije's mouth tugged gently at her neck, and Sasa felt her body come alive under his touch. Her skin burned like it was on fire beneath his fingers as his hand sensually slid down past her collarbone to her breast to pluck a hardened nipple between his fingers. With every drop of blood that left her she was drawn closer to him. She was inside him now, but strangely, she felt him inside her—in her blood. In her mind.

Sasa...you're inside me now. Forever.

His voice whispered in her head, his seductive pledge touching her deep inside. Over and over, his words repeated in her mind, imprinting themselves on her memory.

Sasa knew she should be frightened. A vampire was taking her blood and whispering how she would be inside him forever. The problem was that while he was doing those things he was making love to her like no man ever had.

Pleasure swept over her again as Vasilije pumped faster into her. The room began to swim past her eyes and then she was on her back, gazing up in stunned silence at him. He stared down into her eyes as he hooked his arm under her knee, pulling her leg back and opening her core completely to him. She felt exposed, embarrassed. She barely knew him, and her past history with men hadn't been what anyone would call successful. Hell, it was a train wreck. As her dating history paraded through her mind, just seeing him looking down at her was awkward.

"No," she whispered faintly despite her body wishing he'd never stop his delicious assault.

"Never hide yourself from me, Sasa," he said seductively as his gaze slid slowly from her face to between her legs.

"I..." she began but found she couldn't remember what she wanted to say as he thrust into her again, his body joining with hers completely.

Vasilije was at her neck, and Sasa stiffened in fear at the thought of those razor-sharp fangs sinking into her already tender skin. To her surprise, his lips pressed against her neck just before his fangs began drawing blood, yet all she felt was need for him to be inside her in every way possible.

Something about when he touched her made all the fear and insecurities melt away. Slowly, she felt his fangs slide in, burying themselves in her neck, just before his mouth began drawing from her.

The feeling of him taking from her was like nothing else in the world. It made her head spin and her heart pound, but she wasn't afraid anymore. Only that he would stop and take with him the perfect sensations his mouth was creating in her.

Minutes went by as Sasa held his head to her, the silky black strands of hair gliding through her fingers as she urged him to take more of her. Vasilije at last raised his head and she saw him for what he truly was— vampire. Tiny drops of deep red blood fell from his pure white fangs onto his lips, full and luscious, as he stared down into her eyes. He looked like a wild beast as his tongue slid across his lower lip to catch the drops.

"Sasa."

His voice sounded like she felt. Needy. Needy for him. Needy for more. As he spoke, he slowly moved in and out of her, his cock burying deep inside her and then leaving her empty and wanting him again.

"Listen to your body."

"Vasilije, I... your voice is inside me. I hear you speak to me even when you're silent."

Gently, he pressed his lips to hers and whispered, "Just as you're inside me now, I'm in you."

And then his head was next to hers and his arms held her as each movement he made into her brought her closer to the sweetest surrender.

Her body was his to feast on, his to take his pleasure in. Each thrust of his cock buried him deep in her, touching some spot unknown before him. She wanted more of that sensation—more of him. Her body told him all its secrets and she heard him respond inside her mind.

Let me give you what you crave, Sasa.

Yes. Give me what I crave. Please.

Suddenly, he rose up over her, the picture of power and desire facing her. "Let it take you. Come with me."

Her climax snaked through her core and exploded to every part of her body, overwhelming her senses and mind. Vasilije was everywhere—inside her, above her, next to her, his seductive words echoing inside her head.

Surrender to me, Sasa. Give yourself to me.

She didn't have a choice. The sensations he'd created in her meant she would've begged to give herself to him.

Sasa didn't know if she came for seconds or hours. The feeling took hold of her body and mind, and she was lost to it. All she knew was him.

Vasilije.

And then there was silence.

Sasa opened her eyes at the touch of his tongue to her neck on the spot he'd drunk from. Instantly, her passion bloomed again, and her pussy ran wet with desire.

"Yes," she moaned, eager to experience him again.

Vasilije chuckled softly in her ear. "Not yet, love. You need time to recover."

Sasa turned her head, confused. "Recover? But..."

He stroked her cheek as he propped his head up on his palm. "I took a great deal from you, pet. You're weak. You must rest."

Weak was the last thing she felt. She felt alive.

Sensual. Sexy. More than ever before. And she wanted those feelings to stay with her.

"I'm not tired. I want more," she whispered against his lips. "More."

"I promise you'll have more, love. But now you need to rest."

Sasa accepted the rejection still unsure of why he kept insisting she was tired. When he wrapped his arms around her, she laid her head on his chest, content to listen to his heartbeat until he turned to her again.

In the silence between them, she opened her mind to feel his emotions. She'd sensed happiness from him earlier when she'd agreed to let him take her blood and again when she'd begged him not to stop, but since then the experience had been so overwhelming she'd almost been unsure of her own feelings, never mind his.

As she lay on his chest, Sasa let his emotions come to her. Gradually, a gentle feeling came over her. Sasa was surprised to sense he was peaceful and satisfied.

The idea that she could be a part of that kind of happiness for another soul was all she knew as she closed her eyes to rest.

HOURS LATER, Sasa awoke, still against Vasilije's body. Unsure of what time it was, she quickly dressed. She'd promised her mother she'd visit, and she knew Tatiana was due at her house just after sunset.

Turning the doorknob, Sasa turned to look back at him in the bed where they'd made love for hours. He was deathly still. His black hair, a stark contrast against the white pillow, framed his face, and he was the picture of calm. Slowly, almost imperceptibly, his chest rose and fell with each breath. Did he know she was gone from him now?

Something in him called to her, and she returned to him with a feeling of guilt. For the second time, she'd planned to simply sneak away after their time together, as if she were ashamed. Standing by the side of the bed, she leaned over and lightly kissed his lips. "Goodnight, Vasilije."

A quick note scribbled on some scrap paper and placed on the pillow next to him and she stepped out into the late afternoon sun. By the time she arrived home, the sun was already setting. Nervously, she waited for Tatiana, her mind struggling over the puzzle of why she sought revenge on Vasilije. Had they been something to one another at some point in time? Jealousy spiked in Sasa at just the thought of him with her. Beautiful, sexy, and a vampire, Tatiana was everything she wasn't. Even her name was exotic and sensual. And hers? Sasa said her name in her head and frowned.

Sounds like something a child says. Not regal like hers at all.

In mere minutes, Sasa had constructed an entire relationship between Tatiana and Vasilije, complete with undying devotion and his devastation at losing her, the one true love of his entire existence. Jealousy intermingled with her memories of him making love to her just hours earlier and before she knew it, she'd convinced herself of his complete lack of interest in her, except as a temporary diversion meant to help him forget the pain of losing Tatiana.

Disgusted with her insecurity, Sasa caught herself before she spiraled completed out of control. Yes, it was true she'd never had much success with men. Yes, she'd been cheated on and lied to. And used. But Vasilije had been honest with her from the beginning.

But he also said what we did meant nothing.

Sasa leaned back on the couch and closed her eyes. If only she had a girlfriend to talk to. As she wished for someone to confide in, the reality of the situation returned to her. She was falling for a vampire she barely knew. One who probably had dozens of women he slept with. She was likely just one of many and merely the first he'd have in this part of the world.

Gorgeous men don't fall for just one woman.

Two loud bangs startled her out of her jealous self-loathing, and she quickly made her way to the front door. On the other side stood Tatiana in all her tall, blond, and gorgeous glory.

"Hi," was all Sasa could muster before she turned back toward the couch.

"Empath, you must ask me in, unless we're going to have our meeting out here."

Even her voice sounded regal. Sasa was sure her voice had never sounded that powerful or commanding. And she couldn't even bother to remember her name!

Turning back to face her, she said in disgust, "Sasa. My name is Sasa."

Tatiana's face showed not a hint of embarrassment at hearing Sasa's answer. With more than a bit of irritation, she said, "Yes. I remember. Now are you going to invite me in?"

Sure that was the best she was going to get, Sasa waved her in. "Please come in, Tatiana."

As soon as she crossed the threshold she began her questioning. "What do you have to tell me, Sasa?"

Sasa knew what she wanted to hear. She wanted all the lurid details of Vasilije's misery over the loss of Teagan. She wanted to hear her murder of his vampire had been successful in devastating him.

"Vasilije is in mourning over Teagan. You really hurt him, Tatiana. I can see it in everything he does and hear it in everything he says. He's devastated."

Tatiana's face looked confused. "Vasilije must be getting soft in his old age. Devastated?"

Sasa saw she'd overplayed her description of him a little. Quickly, she tried to recover. "Well, maybe devastated is a bit much. I guess I meant more enraged than devastated."

"Ah, yes. That's my Vasilije. Forever vengeful about something."

As Tatiana sat down in a chair across from her, Sasa repeated her words in her head. *My Vasilije.* Every insecurity from earlier came flooding back, and she had to fight the urge to ask Tatiana exactly how she knew him. And what did she mean by old? How old was he?

"Does he trust you yet? I want him to completely trust you so he senses nothing before I go to him."

"Not yet. It's only been a few days. I think he will, though. As you said, he's old, so that might make him naturally suspicious." Sasa waited a moment and then asked the question she had to know the answer to. "How old is he anyway?"

Unsure if she'd shown the wrong interest in him, she

made her expression as vacant as possible, hoping Tatiana wouldn't see how much she wanted to know the answer. For a second, it seemed as though Tatiana was suspicious of her question, but as quickly as it came it left and she began to talk freely about what she knew.

"He's an old one. Has to be over four hundred now. I met him when he was a brand-new vampire. What fun he was! More than once we enjoyed a night of feeding. So sensual...the vampire you see now is old and cynical, past his prime, but long ago before he turned to picking up prey in nightclubs, he was the one every vampire in England desired."

Before she could stop herself, Sasa quietly murmured, "Oh."

As Tatiana seemed to enjoy a memory of what she'd described, Sasa worked to tamp down the jealousy that threatened to explode out of her. Everything she'd imagined was true. They had been lovers. And by the way Tatiana talked, there had been many others.

"So what have you done to gain his trust, my empath friend?"

God, she hated when she referred to her ability as if that's all she was! An empath, not a woman. Not a person who was so many other things than someone who could sense the emotions of others.

"I listen to him reminisce about his friend. He does that a lot."

Tatiana sat back in her chair obviously pleased by Sasa's report. "You're a very bright girl, Sasa, to have figured out at such a young age one of the most important things about men. They love it when we listen to them. Very bright. I knew Quiterie wouldn't steer me wrong. Just be careful, dear. He can still turn on the charm like few others can. You don't want to find yourself in a compromising position with a vampire like Vasilije."

"Why? Am I in danger?"

Sasa was sure she wasn't, but she was curious to hear Tatiana's opinion.

"Always with vampires there's danger. I could rip your neck apart in a split second and drain you, if I so chose to right now. Vasilije won't hesitate to do just that if he finds out you're spying on him, my dear."

"Oh. Well, I'll be careful."

"And don't let yourself be seduced into bed with him. We can manipulate humans, especially sexually, and you could find yourself in a very dangerous place if you sleep with him."

Sasa didn't hear anything after Tatiana admitted vampires could manipulate humans. It had been some special vampire mojo, after all. She knew she hadn't begun to fall for him on her own.

Tatiana rose to leave and began to make her way to the door. "And just as important, don't let him drink from you."

"Why?"

Sasa regretted asking the question as soon as Tatiana turned around, her expression one of pure suspicion.

"Has he had your blood, Sasa?"

Fighting the impulse to touch the spot where he'd drunk from her, Sasa shook her head. "No. He hasn't even asked."

Tatiana smiled her perfect smile. "Dear, he doesn't need to ask. We can hypnotize you and take what we want." She stood staring at her for what seemed like minutes and then said, "Let me see your neck."

Sasa froze in terror as the woman walked toward her and began examining her neck. In her hurry to get home, she hadn't even looked to see if there was any evidence of what she'd let him do.

Tatiana's long fingers ran up and down the sides of her neck as Sasa silently prayed to God there were no holes or traces of blood left. Each touch made her shiver in fear, but quickly Tatiana seemed satisfied that he'd not tasted her.

Looking into her eyes, Tatiana smiled as she reminded Sasa of the plan. "Remember, you need him to trust you. Keep his attention on you but no sex or blood."

"That might be more difficult now. He's got a new vampire, Jeremy, so he's got to deal with him."

Tatiana raised her eyebrows in surprise. "Jeremy? Hmm...interesting. Well, remember what you're supposed to be doing in exchange for me making your mother better. I'd hate to see her have to go."

Sasa watched as the vampire turned on her heels and left, her thinly veiled threat still hanging in the air. No matter what she claimed about Vasilije, Sasa was surer than ever which one was more dangerous. Now she had to make sure no one she cared about got hurt while she fulfilled her deal with Tatiana.

10

———————

Vasilije watched in confusion as Jeremy primped in the bathroom mirror. Liquids of all different types seemed to be of the utmost importance, if the array of bottles lined up on the counter were any indication.

"Jeremy, how much longer will all this take?"

The brand-new vampire shot him a look of disgust as he continued to fuss with his hair. "You could learn a thing or two from me. Women love this look. They want a man who takes care of himself. That means skin, hair, the works."

Vasilije raised an eyebrow as he compared his look and Jeremy's in the mirror. "Women want a man who spends hours in front of the mirror to look like he just rolled out of bed?"

Undeterred, Jeremy messed the top of his hair. "I'll tell you what, Vasilije. I bet I could get more women tonight than you could. That dark and mysterious look can't stand up to what I've got going on."

The idea that Jeremy's arrogance, ignorance, and

overdone metrosexuality could attract anyone amused Vasilije, and he laughed out loud at the reflection in the mirror. "Some other night, Jeremy, I'll be happy to show you how wrong you are. Tonight, we have work to do, so stop fucking with your hair and meet me outside."

"Okay. Hey, is that girl coming with us? I was hoping to see her again."

Possessiveness raced through Vasilije. "Sasa's mine," he warned.

Jeremy stopped staring at himself and shifted his gaze to the reflection on his right. "Oh, I just figured she was someone we could share. You know, like a vampire thing, since she seemed to want me last night."

"Take this as your only warning. Sasa is not a thing or to be shared."

Jeremy seemed to sulk for a moment but quickly rebounded to finish his hair. "Whatever."

Tired of watching him, Vasilije turned to leave, hoping he'd get the hint. Checking the time, he made his way outside as he wondered if Sasa would show up. Her note had said she had errands to run and to wait for her. Vasilije looked up at the starry night sky, disgusted that in such a short time he'd allowed not one but two others to dictate his comings and goings.

His time as a vampire had been a solitary one, for the most part. Except for a chosen few, those he sired were kept around only as long as necessary and then let out into the world on their own, called back only when he needed them. Favorites like Brandon and Teagan he preferred to keep close because he liked their company, and the females he tended to keep with him for obvious reasons, but they were never permanent, and he liked it that way.

Now he had two new vampires, neither of whom he liked at all, who he looked forward to releasing as soon as possible, and Sasa, a human woman who had somehow become someone who meant something to him. Closing his eyes, Vasilije breathed deeply as he reminisced about ages past, missing the solitude of those days.

He sensed Sasa approach him, smelling the sweet scent of her shampoo as she made her way down the sidewalk. As he opened his eyes, she stopped in front of him and looked up with a quizzical expression on her face.

"What are you doing?"

"Waiting for you, pet."

"Really? You're standing here waiting for me? How long have you been out here?"

"A few minutes."

"Did you know I was coming? Is that some kind of vampire superpower you guys have?"

Vasilije smiled. "Superpower? No. And I didn't know you were coming now, but your note indicated you'd be back. Now all we have to do is wait for Jeremy."

Sasa's curious appearance vanished, replaced by a look of pain. "Oh, he's coming?"

"He has to. He's too new to be left alone."

In some tiny spot in his mind, Vasilije was happy to see her unhappiness at the news she had to spend time with Jeremy.

"Any chance he doesn't remember last night?"

Shaking his head, Vasilije saw what was bothering

her. "Don't worry. I already explained about you to him. I'm his sire, so he won't be a problem."

Sasa turned her head but began to speak. "I'm a little embarrassed about that. I can't believe I did that. Or..."

Vasilije took her chin between his thumb and fore-finger to make her face him. "Look at me, love. Or what?"

She slowly opened her eyes and looked up into his. "Or that I let you bite me and drink my blood."

"Do you wish you hadn't?"

Sasa sighed. "No, but...Vasilije, do you have some kind of vampire mojo or something that makes me want to do things with you?"

Shaking his head, he chuckled. "No, not unless I hypnotize you."

"Well, I know you can't do that, so it must be something else."

Humming at the thought that she couldn't be brought under his spell, he considered trying again, nonetheless, but Sasa continued talking.

"I just don't understand why then."

"Why what, love?"

"I don't just jump into bed with men. I mean, I'm not a virgin, but I've never been one to sleep with a man so quickly."

Vasilije couldn't imagine Teagan waiting very long to sleep with any woman, even Sasa. "I'm sure it's because I'm a vampire. It probably went the same way with Teagan."

Sasa shook her head. "No, we knew each other for almost a month."

"Really?"

As Sasa explained how they met and their first

month together, Vasilije considered the possibility that he really didn't know the man his friend had become in his time in New Orleans. In the hundred years he'd known him, never had Teagan been willing to wait a month to bed a woman. In fact, he'd outdone Vasilije on many occasions when it came to their conquests. True, there had been a few he'd technically courted as more than one-night stands, but even those never took a month.

Perhaps Teagan had truly been in love with Sasa, and despite his cheating, had seen her as the one he'd wanted to sire. That could explain his waiting a month to sleep with her. Or maybe he had an old-fashioned streak in him that only she brought out.

Or perhaps Sasa wasn't what she claimed to be.

A hand came down on Vasilije's shoulder and he turned to see Jeremy, all ready for his evening out, standing next to him. "Let's roll. Where we headed?"

"To the Quarter. The vampires there might have some more information about who killed Teagan."

Sasa's face looked like the picture of concern. "The Quarter? Is this going to be like our visit to the Archon? Maybe I shouldn't go."

Vasilije studied her closely, more suspicious than he preferred. Now she didn't want to go hunting Teagan's killer?

"Don't worry, love. You'll be safe. None of those vampires are as old as I am, and Jeremy will help if there's a problem. I need you to look for the person who did this."

"Yeah, and no need to worry," Jeremy chimed in. "Even if Vasilije can't handle them, I got you, sweetheart."

Irritated by his new vampire yet once again, Vasilije groaned and began walking. "Let's go."

THE FRENCH QUARTER buzzed with activity with people packed tightly against one another. Vasilije watched Jeremy carefully as he snaked his way toward the first place he could get a drink. Sasa held his arm tightly as they weaved through the crowd and followed the younger vampire.

Vasilije saw fear on her face now. Leaning down, he said loudly next to her ear, "You live here. Why do you seem so uncomfortable in the French Quarter?"

Sasa moved her head side to side as she watched the mass of revelers near them. "I don't like crowds. I feel uncomfortable in them."

Squeezing his arm tighter, she said, "Is the place we have to go nearby?"

He sensed her discomfort and pulled her toward a spot where the crowd had thinned. Gently, he pushed her back against the wall and looked down at her face. Fuck, she did something to him that made him not only possessive of her but protective too. Whatever it was, it made him want to take her into his arms and kiss away all her fears.

Out of the crowd, he could speak in his normal tone. "Sasa, I won't let anyone or anything hurt you. I'd sooner stake one like me before seeing you harmed."

Sasa stared up at him with wide eyes. "Please tell me you put some kind of spell or something on me. Tell me there's a reason why every time you're this close to me I want you more than I've ever wanted any other man."

Her words hit him deep inside and made his cock stiffen hard as a rock. The thought of being inside her right then made his mind race with possibilities. Unable to stop himself, he dipped his head down to let his mouth softly touch hers and slid his tongue between her lips.

Sasa arched her body toward his and tugged on his hair passionately. Tiny, whimpering sounds escaped her mouth as she returned his kiss with desire that only aroused him more.

Reluctantly, Vasilije pulled away and cradled Sasa's face in his hands. "Love, there's no spell. And as much as I want to be buried inside you up to my balls right now, we can't. Jeremy can't be left alone here, and we need to find out who killed one of my vampires."

"I know and I'm sorry. I don't know what's wrong with me."

Tracing her lower lip with his thumb, he whispered next to her ear, "There's nothing wrong with you. When we finish here, I promise to show you just how much effect you have on me."

He kissed her and took her hand to lead her to where Jeremy had gone. The fear he'd sensed earlier was gone, and by the time they found the younger vampire, she was giving him the run-down of the Quarter's history.

As they entered the bar, Vasilije spied Jeremy attempting to charm some redhead. Her body language told him he wasn't interrupting anything serious, and tapping him on the shoulder, he reminded him of why they were there.

"I'm busy. Can't you do it without me?" Jeremy whined.

Looking past him, Vasilije saw an empty bar stool. "You're not busy now. Let's go."

Jeremy made his usual sulking expression and followed Vasilije and Sasa outside. "Dude, you're such a cock block. I'm never going to get laid with you around."

Growling, Vasilije said, "Just follow me and keep your mouth shut."

THE BUILDING that housed the French Quarter vampires looked like any other in the Quarter. Two stories with a balcony, it had black painted wrought iron metalwork along the roof, the architectural effect broken up by hanging plants in full bloom. The door on the ground floor was painted a turquoise blue and appeared as festive as everywhere else that surrounded the place.

Vasilije squeezed Sasa's hand and turned to face her. "Don't be frightened. They're just like me."

Sasa smiled. "Got it. Just follow you and keep my mouth shut."

Groaning, he turned back to face the door. "That mouth is going to get you in trouble, love."

"Promises, promises, Vasilije."

Vasilije drew up the heavy door knocker and banged it against the door twice. He hoped these vampires would be as willing to help as last time. The leader, a vampire named LeClerc, had left a message saying he had what might be a lead about Teagan's killer. Maybe he'd found out something more by now.

A tall, bleach blonde female answered the door in nothing but beads and a g-string. Sasa's hand tightened its grip on his hand and before Jeremy could say anything, Vasilije shot him a look and mouthed, "Keep your mouth shut."

"We're here to see LeClerc."

"Hon, that's a damn shame. I've got beads to give out and you're just the man I'd like to give 'em to."

Before Vasilije could politely decline, the blonde spun on her four-inch heels and began leading them to the back of the building. He knew Sasa's eyes were boring holes through him and as the three of them walked, he turned to see her eyebrows raised in a look that seemed to accuse him of something.

"Something wrong?"

With a big smile, she said, "Seems I'm not the only one you have an effect on."

Leaning down next to her ear, he said, "I may be reaching here, but I'd guess every man has that effect on her. Even Jeremy wouldn't strike out with her."

"Thanks, man. But you'd probably cock block me on her too."

Vasilije shot Jeremy another threatening look and turned back to see the blonde had led them to the room he'd visited his last time there. LeClerc sat at a table with three other vampires drinking and playing cards. He stood to welcome them, and Vasilije shook his hand.

"Thanks for seeing us."

"Sit. Can Yvette get you anything?" LeClerc asked referring to the almost naked woman who'd escorted them there.

"No, thanks."

As he, Sasa, and Jeremy sat on a couch near the table, Vasilije quickly scanned the room, just in case this group of vampires had ideas like the Archon had about humans. Other than the three average sized males who sat with LeClerc and Yvette, two other females sat on another couch at the other end of the room. As of yet, no one seemed to care that Sasa wasn't like them, but he knew that could change in a flash.

"I'm glad you came. After you left the last time, I put some feelers out to see if anyone knew anything about your man. I got nothing until last night. You know anyone named Jasper?"

"No."

"Any chance your man did?"

Vasilije tried to imagine what someone named Jasper looked like. He could imagine one of the Swamprats being named Jasper, but would Teagan have known any vampires from that group?

"I don't know." Turning to Sasa, he asked, "Did Teagan know anyone named Jasper?"

Sasa shook her head and leaned in toward him to whisper, "I don't know if I can be of any help. While we were having troubles...well, I didn't see as much of him. He might have met someone then. I just don't know. I'm sorry."

"It's okay. Just try to think if you ever remember that name."

"I don't. I'm sorry."

Vasilije turned back to LeClerc. "We don't know if Teagan knew any Jasper."

LeClerc dealt a hand of poker and sat back to study his cards. "Well, that's the name I hear might know something about your vamp. Seems he heard about someone getting staked a few nights back. I don't know if that's your man, but it's worth a shot."

"Do you know anything about him?"

Vasilije waited as LeClerc and his vampires bet and took their cards. Another bet and a call and LeClerc was ready to focus on their conversation again. "Other than he's not one of us, all I know is his first name and where to find him. Wish I could help more."

"No, you've been a big help. Thanks."

LeClerc folded and threw his cards down in disgust on the table. "Yvette, bring me the address of that Jasper guy."

Happy to have something to go on, Vasilije took the address from Yvette and prepared to leave. Leaning over him, intentionally dangling her breasts just an inch away from his mouth, Yvette eyed Sasa, and he tensed for what might be a problem.

"You look familiar, hon. Where do I know you from?"

Leaning back, he looked at Sasa's surprised face. It seemed impossible that she'd know Yvette, but then again, she had been a vampire's girlfriend.

"Oh, no. I'm sorry. I don't think we've ever met," Sasa answered, her voice shaky.

"I'm sure I've seen you somewhere before. You from around here?"

"Yes. I bet you just think you saw me because I'm pretty common looking. You know, brown hair and brown eyes. Very average."

Yvette stood up again and Vasilije took that as their cue to leave. Before he could take a step, though, Yvette yelled, "Quiterie's! That's where I know you from. You're Sasa, the voodoo lady's friend."

Vasilije turned back to look at Sasa and saw the blood drain from her face. Voodoo?

11

Sasa looked around at each of the faces that stared at her. The vampire LeClerc, with his long black hair and almost comical, precisely shaped moustache, seemed amused by the revelation that Yvette had just announced. His broad smile lit up his face and more than before, he looked like one of the performers common to the Quarter. Yvette seemed pleased by what she surely saw was recognition in her eyes. Sasa had recognized her at the door and had hoped to escape without her figuring out who she was.

And Vasilije. His icy blue eyes stared at her in suspicion almost telegraphing the question he must have been asking himself. *How does Sasa know a voodoo priestess?*

How would she explain her relationship with Quiterie?

Her mind raced as his blue eyes stared intently into hers. With little effort, she sensed his confusion but was happy to know he wasn't angry. Yet.

"Sasa was Teagan's girlfriend. It's been hard on her dealing with the loss."

Stunned by Vasilije's sympathetic words, Sasa stared at him as she heard LeClerc ask, "And now she's yours?"

"She's my responsibility. As Teagan's sire, I have to ensure she's protected. I owe that to him."

She'd been wrong. Vasilije's anger came at her in waves now, despite the calm tone in his voice.

"I understand. That's what I'd do if one of mine was staked. It's how Yvette came to me."

Yvette sat down on LeClerc's lap and kissed him. As Sasa silently pleaded with her eyes for Vasilije to take her out of there, he took her by the hand, said his goodbyes, and led her out to the street.

Jeremy came up behind them on the sidewalk. "Voodoo? Wow! You're one interesting girl."

"Jeremy, go back to the house now."

Vasilije's voice was as hard as stone and even Jeremy seemed to understand not to anger him more. Without a word, he turned toward the direction of the house and walked away.

"I can explain, Vasilije."

He said nothing, instead roughly taking her by the arm and leading her into the crowd. Sasa followed him, sensing the anger growing inside him by the minute. Worse, beneath the anger was hurt. She felt it and winced in pain as it touched her inside.

If he'd just give her a chance, she could explain. At least in part. He had every reason to be angry. It was true. She had lied to him, but that was before she knew him.

Sasa knew that wasn't entirely true, no matter how much she wanted to convince herself it was. She'd been lying to him from the moment she'd met him. What choice did she have? Tatiana had lived up to her part of their deal. Her mother was no longer sick and dying. So now she had to live up to her part of the bargain—even if it ate at her every moment of the day.

Turning onto a side street, Sasa prayed he'd listen to what she had to say. She may not be able to tell him the entire truth, but she needed him to know that she wasn't the liar he thought she was.

Vasilije spun her around and pushed her hard against the cement wall of a building. Stunned, she heard the click as his fangs slammed into his mouth and saw the rage in his eyes, making them look colder than ever before.

"You've got one chance to explain what's going on before I drain you, my dear Sasa."

"Vasilije, it's not what you think."

Ominously, he leaned in toward her neck and grazed his fangs across her skin. "I'm running out of patience, love."

"Please listen. Please."

He pulled back from her and stood staring at her angrily. Fighting back tears, Sasa hoped he remembered what he'd said the last time they stood like this.

"I do know Quiterie. She helps me with my mother. You see, mama's sick and I couldn't stand to see her in pain anymore. So I went to Quiterie for something to take her pain away. And then I had to go back again and again because she always got worse again. I couldn't afford to pay her, so I agreed to help her by using my talent."

"Which is?"

"I'm an empath."

Vasilije stood still as a stone staring at her and then squinted his eyes angrily. "You're lying."

"No. I admit I lied by not telling you, but I really am an empath. I can prove it."

He released her shoulders and stepped back from her. "How?"

"I know what you're feeling right now."

"Pet, you'd have to be blind or stupid not to know what I'm feeling right now. You'll have to do better, Sasa."

Tentatively, she reached out to place her hand on his chest above his heart and opened herself up to let in the hurt and betrayal he felt. "I'm sorry I hurt you."

He pulled her hand from him and pushed her away. "Nice trick, but you're wrong. You couldn't hurt me. Now get the fuck away from me before I follow through on my threat and drain you right here."

Sasa grabbed his arm as he turned to walk away from her. Spinning back to face her, he showed none of the kindness she'd seen in him before.

"Please, Vasilije. You have to believe me. I didn't mean to hurt you."

Opening his mouth a sliver, he showed her the tip of his fangs. "You better hope this Quiterie backs up your story or the next time I won't let you go."

His emotions hit her squarely in the chest and she backed up away from him. Her head hung, she said quietly, "I'm sorry. Please forgive me."

"Get away from me."

Sasa dropped his sleeve and watched in misery as he walked away. As much as she wanted to curl up and die from the sadness she'd felt from him, she had to get to Quiterie and warn her. The voodoo shop was only a few blocks away, so she set out hurriedly, hoping to get there before he did. While she walked, she called the voodoo priestess but each time got her voicemail.

Pressing redial, she snapped, "Fucking Quiterie! You're lucky if he doesn't drain you tonight."

Again the voodoo priestess's voicemail came through the phone. "Quiterie, it's Sasa. Call me the second you get this."

Jamming the phone into her pocket, Sasa made her way through the drunken crowd on Bourbon Street, bouncing off people and even a light post before the throng of people thinned out and she was once again alone. Not that being alone was what she wanted.

The memory of the hurt in Vasilije's eyes tore at her heart. Would he ever forgive her? Would he ever again be that man who promised to protect her and swore he'd stake one of his own to ensure she wasn't harmed? Sadly, she admitted to herself he wouldn't when he found out virtually everything about her had been a lie, and worse yet, she'd played a part in Teagan's murder.

How had everything spun so out of control?

Quiterie's shop on Iberville was dark when she arrived, and Sasa prayed to God she would call before Vasilije could find her. As she turned to leave, she ran headlong into Tatiana, who stood directly in her path.

"Having a lovely night out?" she asked in her usual voice that made Sasa instantly uneasy.

"Just another night in the Quarter, I guess." Sasa hoped she didn't see the emotions she was fighting to control as she steadied herself on her feet.

"Looking for our friend, Quiterie? She seems to be out for the evening."

Hopefully, she wasn't out permanently. Sasa smiled nervously. "You haven't seen her tonight?"

Twirling her long blond hair around her finger, Tatiana shook her head. "No, but I wasn't looking for her. Why are you looking for her, Sasa?"

Fear bubbling up inside her, Sasa wondered if Tatiana had run into Vasilije as he was looking for Quiterie. Had she gotten her revenge already?

"Just in the neighborhood, I guess, so I thought I'd say hi."

Tatiana leaned in toward her and her fangs slowly dropped into her mouth. "I would think you'd have better things to do with your time than look for our voodoo friend. How are you doing with Vasilije?"

"Fine. Just fine. I have to go now, Tatiana. He's expecting me and I don't want to give him any reason to think something's wrong."

Sasa turned to walk away, but the vampire caught her by the sleeve. "Take care, Sasa. I'll be coming to see you soon."

———

EACH STEP he took away from Sasa made the anger that raged inside him worse. He should have known there was something off about her. Every time he was near her she seemed to know just what he was feeling. Even when he was sure he'd stuffed his emotions down where no other being could know they existed, she knew.

It had been nice having someone who understood. Now it felt like shit knowing she'd lied to him about who she was.

Vasilije cringed at the anger that swirled inside him. He could handle lies from women he didn't give a fuck about, but from the few who he'd let in, they hurt worse than almost any other pain.

That was the problem. He'd let her in. Hundreds of years and just as many women should have taught him not to, but he had.

No wonder Teagan loved her.

What Vasilije needed now was information from Jasper, a stiff drink, and a soft woman, in that order. The Jasper part wasn't too far away, if he was gauging the directions correctly, and then the drink and the woman would soon follow. Then he'd check out Sasa's story with the voodoo lady.

Fuck. He didn't want to think of Sasa anymore. Not until he'd had the drink, at least.

The address LeClerc had given him was in the Irish Channel section and Vasilije saw instantly as he entered the area that this wasn't the New Orleans the tourism board put on the brochures. Wrought iron and lavish galleries overlooking busy streets lit up in neon lights were replaced by one-story shotgun houses that teetered on dilapidation.

He stopped under a flickering streetlight to check that the address on the paper in his hand matched the numbers on the house in front of him.

2730.

Vasilije stepped up the two broken concrete steps to the door and knocked. As he waited for someone to answer, he studied the structure in front of him. No more than twelve feet wide, the green painted house resembled something closer to a storage container. Compared to his house in London or Teagan's in the Garden District, this looked like someplace someone down on his luck would stay.

It looked like a Jasper's house.

No one answered his second knock, so he made his way around to the back of the tiny, narrow house and climbed the rickety wooden stairs to the back door. Peering through the dirty glass window, he saw nothing but darkness.

"Fuck. Well, I'll be back for you, Jasper."

He let the screen door slam closed and stepped onto the stairs, but before his foot could hit the second one, something attacked him, taking him to the ground.

"Who are you? What's your name?"

His attacker wasn't big, but he was fast. However, contrary to popular belief, size always trumped speed, especially when size can pin speed to the ground. Rolling the man over, Vasilije pressed all his weight into his arms and hands and forced him against the concrete.

"Settle down and I'll let you go, Jasper."

The man beneath his hold looked up in surprise. "How do you know who I am?"

"Let's just say you seem like a Jasper."

Vasilije studied the face of his would-be informant. Dirty blond hair hung to his shoulders in what looked like greasy clumps. Jasper looked like he hadn't seen a razor in days, and Vasilije guessed it had been at least that long since he'd had a bath, if the sickening smell wafting up to his nostrils was any indication.

"You gonna let me up? Or are we stayin like this all night?"

Getting back to his feet, Vasilije looked down as

Jasper sat up, slid his hands through his hair, and sprung to his feet. Pushing past him, the man climbed the stairs and walked into the house with Vasilije following behind.

In the light, the inside of the house looked as run down as it did outside. Partially chipped plaster and paint marked the walls and everything, including the white paint that remained, seemed to have a yellow-brownish haze over it. Jasper took a seat on an old red and yellow plaid couch and lit a cigarette as he gestured for Vasilije to sit down.

"Take a load off."

Looking around at his choices, Vasilije spied a chair that matched the couch in pattern and age and an old milk crate.

"Thanks. I'm good. I just need some information."

Jasper shrugged and took a deep drag of his cigarette. "Suit yourself. Sorry about that out there. I didn't know who you were. Coulda been a bad man."

"I still could be."

"Nah. I got a sense from you while you were makin me part of the sidewalk."

Is this town full of empaths?

"Do you know what I am?"

Jasper butted out his cigarette and sat back to study Vasilije. "Other than a vamp, what else do I need to know? You feelin hungry?"

The thought of putting his lips against Jasper's greasy skin make Vasilije's stomach turn, and he grimaced in disgust. "No thanks."

"Hell, I wasn't offerin. I have no interest in you drinkin from me like a damn Coca-Cola. What kind of information you lookin for?"

"Someone killed one of my vampires. I hear you may know something about it."

Jasper nervously lit another cigarette. "Now I think I am gettin a bad man vibe from you. I didn't see anything. Sorry, I can't help you."

Vasilije opened his mouth and let his fangs snap into place. The terrified look on Jasper's face told him the effect had worked.

"Jasper, I'm going to ask one more time before I sink my teeth into your neck and bleed you dry. What do you know about a vampire getting killed a few nights ago?"

Two deep drags burned the cigarette down to the filter and Jasper began to backpedal on his earlier statement. "Okay, okay. I...I might be able to help you. You don't have to fuckin threaten to kill me. Who's your friend?"

"Teagan Collins."

"Okay, okay. That sounds like a name I wouldn't forget. What's your name?"

"Vasilije."

"Just Vasilije? Like Madonna?"

"No, nothing like Madonna. Stop stalling. What do you know?"

Another cigarette made its way to Jasper's mouth. "You heard right. I did hear about a vamp getting staked the other night. I mentioned it to one of the vamps that hangs out at the Channel Bar. But I don't know the guy's name that got it."

"What do you know?"

Jasper's hands began to shake, and the ash from his cigarette fell onto the dirty coffee table in front of him. "A friend of mine said he was at a lady's house the other night and heard some kind of ruckus two doors down where his lady said a vamp lived. Something like someone really screaming up a storm. At first he thought it could be some guy and his lady gettin their freak on. You know how some ladies get like that when it gets all hot and heavy."

Vasilije's impatience began to get the better of him and he took a step toward the couch and growled.

"Okay, okay. I guess maybe someone like you doesn't get that kind of lady."

"Move on with the story."

"Okay, okay. So my buddy stepped out onto the porch —he was over in the Garden District—and listened for a bit. Seems whoever it was screaming was mighty upset about something having to do with another guy."

"Did your friend hear any names?"

Jasper shook his head quickly. "No. No names. But he said there was a lady with them. She didn't say anything, though."

"Go on."

"He saw what they looked like. The lady had dark hair and the other one was tall and blond."

"Jasper, I need to know if the blond was a woman."

"He didn't know. He only saw the guy and the blond through a window. The brunette was out on the porch so he could see her."

"Which one staked him?"

"My buddy said all of a sudden the yelling between them stopped and the one on the porch screamed. She ran inside and my buddy heard nothing else."

Vasilije's mind raced as he processed everything Jasper was saying. Sasa had said the guy who staked

Teagan was blond and she'd have been the woman Jasper's friend had seen outside on the porch. But it didn't sound like the blond was a man now.

"Anything else?"

"No. He got the hell out of there and quick."

"I need to know exactly where he was that night. Where can I find the Channel Bar?"

Jasper shook his head. "No good. Slaney don't hang out at the Channel, and I haven't seen him since then. I'm worried one of you got to him. I should never said anything."

Vasilije knew there was no more to get from Jasper. He was convinced his friend had seen the person who'd staked Teagan. Even more, he was convinced he needed to find Sasa and ask her again what happened that night.

"Take care, Jasper. And you might want to take it easy on those. They're going to kill you."

Lighting up, he smiled. "If one of you don't first."

12

Even though she knew she shouldn't, Sasa let her feet guide her back to Teagan's. The way things had been left with Vasilije bothered her. Yes, she'd hid her ability from him, but not to hurt him. She needed him to know that.

She knew it would be worse if he found out she was supposed to be helping Tatiana, but that was a problem she'd deal with when the time came. Now she just needed him to know what he thought about her was wrong.

One dim light illuminated the front window of the house, and Sasa stood out on the street watching for any sign of Vasilije inside. A figure moved behind the curtains, but she couldn't make out who it was.

"No matter," she mumbled. "I'll wait. I have nowhere to be," she admitted sadly.

Remembering the last time she tried to sneak in unannounced, she knocked on the door and then entered, calling out Vasilije's name.

"He's not here, but come in. I'm bored and you can keep me company since I'm stuck here until he comes back."

Sasa sat down in the chair opposite from the couch where Jeremy lay in a t-shirt and pair of jeans. For someone who was new to his surroundings, he seemed comfortable. His shoes were off, and he was barefoot as he relaxed on the couch. She, on the other hand, was distinctly uncomfortable, her actions the other night still a source of embarrassment.

"He hasn't come back yet?"

Had he gone to find the lead LeClerc gave him, or had he found Quiterie?

"No, and I'm sick and fucking tired of waiting around for him."

Sasa calculated the time since he'd left her and hoped Quiterie had stayed away from the shop like she usually did late at night.

Jeremy sat up and leaned forward. "So what's up with you two?"

"Up?"

"Yeah. Like are you his girlfriend or what? You're not one of us, so I know he isn't your sire too. So why are you hanging out with an old vampire?"

Sasa chuckled. Jeremy was so new to this even she knew more about vampires than he did. "Maybe I'm his bleeder."

"What's that?"

"A human who a vampire keeps around to give him blood when none of his own vampires are around."

Jeremy's face was a mixture of curiosity and intense interest. "Are you?"

Shaking her head, Sasa smiled. "No. I was just teasing."

His curiosity sated, he sat back on the couch looking almost disappointed at her answer. "So what is it with you?"

Sasa wasn't sure how to answer his question. Would she be considered his girlfriend? Should she call him her lover? Lover sounded so sophisticated and while Vasilije could definitely be that, Sasa didn't think her run-of-the-mill look measured up.

"We spend time together. I'm helping him find Teagan's killer."

"Yeah? And how's that going?"

She definitely didn't want to get into that conversation in case she slipped up and said something she shouldn't. No, she needed to keep any conversation with Jeremy to topics a frat boy type would like.

"Where are you from, Jeremy?"

"Ruston. Man, I hadn't even thought about home since he turned me. Fuck. I wonder if anyone misses me."

"Sorry. I didn't mean to bring up a sore point."

Shaking his head, he shrugged. "No, no problem. I guess I just always thought vampires lived hotter lives than this. Instead, my life now isn't even half as exciting as it was back in Ruston."

"Oh? What was your life like?"

"You know. A girlfriend. Parties. The usual for someone my age. Now I'm a twenty-one-year-old vampire and I don't get any action because of Big Daddy vamp."

Sasa wasn't sure what to say. Jeremy's life sounded nothing like hers had been for years. He talked of parties and sex, and she considered life to be one responsibility after another. Not that she minded, necessarily, but everything he seemed to miss seemed so foreign to her.

Jeremy appeared lost in his own self-pity, and Sasa took the break in the conversation to truly look at him, something she hadn't done before. He looked like every twenty-something jock type she'd seen in her life. His brown hair was cut to look disheveled, no matter how much a girlfriend fussed with it, but she was sure the effect was anything but randomly casual and more likely the result of far too much time in front of the bathroom mirror. No doubt one touch of his hair would tell the whole story of how laid back his look really was.

He wasn't bad looking, though, and Sasa imagined there were quite a few women—and men—who fought for his attention. As with other self-involved young men, he looked like he spent hours in the gym each day, and his work had paid off. Even through his t-shirt she could see his six-pack. And his arms weren't bad either.

"Jeremy, how did you become a vampire?"

The look of surprise he shot her made Sasa feel uncomfortable. Maybe it was impolite to ask vampires this. As his expression morphed into something more relaxed, she had a sense she'd made a serious mistake by sitting with this vampire.

Sasa stood to leave. "I'm sorry, Jeremy. I didn't mean to pry. I'm going to go now."

Two steps toward the door were all she got before he grabbed her from behind, yanking her back to meet his body. Abs she'd just admired a minute earlier pressed into her back, and his arms held her tightly to him.

"You are a curious one, Sasa. Always asking questions. Does Vasilije like that?"

Jeremy's voice was a mere whisper, but the threatening undertone was unmistakable.

"Please let me go. I meant no harm. If I offended you, I'm sorry, Jeremy."

As one arm pressed heavily across her breasts, another moved toward her neck, and he wrapped his hand around it. As he spoke, he slowly squeezed against her throat, terrifying her.

"Sasa. He does like you, doesn't he? Why is that? No one else seems to please him as much as you do."

Her pulse raced against his fingers as her panic grew by the moment. Jeremy was a new vampire with very little restraint, and his sire was nowhere to be found. If he was hungry and needed to feed, he wouldn't think twice before sinking his teeth into her. But as young as he was, he wouldn't have the necessary restraint to stop before he drained her. Sasa feared in no time at all, he could literally devour her and no one would be able to save her.

Struggling to control her fear, she pleaded, "Jeremy, please let me go."

"I don't think so. I want some, and he's not here to stop me this time."

Jeremy's hand left her neck and quickly moved to between her legs. Before she could push him away, he was beneath her skirt burrowing under her panties. It wasn't just blood he wanted!

"No!" Sasa repeated it over and over as she struggled to wriggle out of his hold, but neither her words nor her actions stopped him. If anything, they seemed to spur him on.

"Wild girl, huh?"

Jeremy pushed her toward the wall and plastered his

body to hers, pinning her in place. Far stronger, he held her still as she heard him unzip his jeans. "Let's see what Big Daddy likes about you, Sasa."

His hand tugged at her skirt, pulling it up over her hips. Sasa tried to turn her head to look for an escape, but he held her to the wall, her eyes filled with the white expanse in front of her. Behind her, his erection pressed into between her cheeks.

"Stop! Let me go, Jeremy!"

Just as she braced for his final assault, a growl like that of an animal's came from behind her, followed by the vicious click of fangs. Horrified, Sasa stiffened and waited.

Suddenly, Jeremy was no longer behind her. Pulling her skirt down over her hips, she turned and saw Vasilije hurl Jeremy across the room into a table that broke into a dozen pieces under his weight. Sasa watched in stunned silence as Vasilije morphed into a terrifying version of himself. As if he were out of control, he raced over to an almost unconscious Jeremy and grabbed him by the collar, jerking him upright. His eyes appeared to be on fire, the icy blue replaced by blood red, and a low growl emanated from somewhere deep inside him.

When he said Jeremy's name, Vasilije's voice seethed his rage. As he flung the young vampire against the wall, his ancient strength seemed to surprise even Jeremy, whose face showed clearly he understood he'd made a mistake with her.

Vasilije turned to face Sasa, and for the first time she witnessed everything he'd become. Horrified, she ran out the door, afraid to look back.

"Sasa's mine."

Vasilije watched as Sasa bolted from the house in fear of him. Turning back to deal with Jeremy, he saw the insolent face of the vampire who'd almost raped and drunk from her staring back at him.

"Sorry, old man. I thought she was for both of us."

As Jeremy spoke, he appeared to almost sneer at Vasilije.

"Both of us?" he hissed as he pushed against his back into the wall.

"Yeah. You know. A bleeder."

The thought of Sasa as anyone's bleeder, even his own, enraged him and the desire to rip Jeremy in two surged through him. "Sasa is not a bleeder. And she's nothing to you."

"I get that, but I'm stuck here all the time. I need some kind of action."

Vasilije pushed Jeremy's head into the wall, grinding his cheek against the drywall. As a fellow vampire—as his sire—he was supposed to care more for him than some human. Somewhere deep inside he knew that, but at that moment it took every ounce of restraint not to shun him, leaving him to possibly die in the world of vampires he wasn't yet ready for.

Every word that came from his mouth made the urge harder to deny.

"What you need is to stop talking, Jeremy."

"But I'm stuck here and it smells like fucking smoke. And all the guy who used to be here drank was Guinness, for Christ's sake! That shit's nasty. And all the while you get to plow her, I get nothing."

"Get the fuck out, Jeremy!"

Vasilije backed away from him and waited as he slowly turned around. Never in the hundreds of years had he ever abandoned one of his vampires. And not because it was against what some Archon or magistrate had decided eons ago. Never once had he left one of his own to find their way in the world before they were ready because they were his. His vampires.

But this one, like Alex, was a mistake.

Jeremy spun around and reacted first with happiness at what he thought was a reprieve, his frat boy look beaming at Vasilije. Then his face grew serious as he understood what his sire had actually said.

"What do you mean?"

Vasilije let his body fall into the chair and closed his eyes. "I mean I'm done with you. Get the fuck out."

"But don't I need to stay with you for a little longer? Isn't that what you said yesterday?"

His eyes still closed, Vasilije didn't say a word. With his hand, he merely waved Jeremy away, as if he were a stranger who was no longer welcome in his presence.

"Whatever. Fine. I don't need you. There are other vampires in this city."

The image of Yvette flashed through Vasilije's mind, followed by LeClerc staking Jeremy after the first time he touched her. Not even that could make him keep him around, though.

Jeremy was still spouting off about how much better his life as a vampire would be as he stuffed bags of chips and pretzels into a bag with his clothes when Vasilije heard something that made him sit up and pay attention.

"...and I'm sure she won't mind having me around."

Vasilije stood up quickly and faced Jeremy. "What did you say?"

Still looting the kitchen, he answered, "I said you're not the only vampire in New Orleans. And I'm sure the vampire I met the other night will be happy to have me stay with her."

"Who?"

"Nobody you'd know."

Quickly losing his patience, Vasilije rushed Jeremy, who was now rifling through Teagan's CDs, throwing the garbage bag full of food and clothes off to the side near the broken table. "Who?"

"Stop crowding me! Fine. Her name is Tatiana. And you should see her. She's a whole lot fucking hotter than that mousy twat of yours."

The name rang in Vasilije's ears. Tatiana. She was in New Orleans. In a flash, his hand shot out and grabbed Jeremy's neck as he slammed him against the wall.

"When? When did you meet her?"

Jeremy's arms flailed as he fought to breathe. Although he knew a vampire couldn't die by strangulation, Vasilije loosened his grip and barked, "Talk!"

"The other night. At the bar, before you two came in."

"Tell me what you know about her!"

Choking, Jeremy coughed out the words, "Blond babe. Hot. And she has a cool accent."

Everything Vasilije had considered impossible became suddenly more than just possible. Tatiana was in

New Orleans. Had she staked Teagan in retaliation for Alex? His mind raced back to Sasa's description of Teagan's killer.

A man.

Had she lied about that too?

"What else do you know about her?" he bellowed as he slammed Jeremy against the wall again.

"Nothing. She just knew I was a vampire. No, I do know something else. Sasa knows her. I saw her with Tatiana in the Quarter after you sent me home."

Vasilije's rage took over and all he could think of was how stupid he'd been. Everything with Sasa had been a lie. Tatiana had murdered his vampire. And Sasa knew it.

Blinded by rage, he grabbed a long piece of wood from the broken pieces of table and held it tightly in his hand, his arm cocked back behind him. The jagged wooden tip pointed toward Jeremy's heart like an arrow seeking a bull's eye.

"Vasilije, no! I'm sorry. I didn't want to hurt her. I just went a little nuts—stir crazy from being stuck here. Don't do this. I'm one of you. She's nothing but a human…"

He didn't hear anything after that. His ears rang with the words, "She's nothing" over and over and then he plunged the stake into Jeremy's heart in the very spot he knew would finish him.

In seconds, Jeremy was no more, and a pile of dust began to settle at Vasilije's feet, particles of his former vampire clinging to his hair and clothes on their way to the floor. Vasilije breathed heavily as the realization of what he'd done came over him. Never before had he killed one of his vampires, one he'd sired.

Now he was no different than Tatiana.

Sickened, he tossed the stake to the pile of wood that had been the table and focused his mind on the one he needed to find.

Sasa.

13

She knew he was nearby. It wasn't her ability as an empath that told her. It was something more. Something deep inside her connected to him. He was inside her, just as he'd promised the night she'd first given her blood to him.

She knew she should fear him. What he'd been at Teagan's was his true self. Vampire. Killer. But it was no use.

Sasa's body came alive at the idea of him coming to her. Every inch of her called out to him. He was like a drug she craved. Outside, she heard silence, but she was drawn to the door as if he were silently willing her to him.

Looking out into the darkness, she closed her eyes and waited. Waited for his touch. For the taste of his lips on hers, his tongue caressing hers as it slid into her mouth. For the feel of his fangs as they first touched her skin in that long moment before he sank into her.

"Sasa."

His voice covered her, seeping into her soul. Slowly, she opened her eyes to see him there. Vasilije. Vampire. He stood still, looking into her eyes as if he were searching for some answer. Blue eyes that seemed to be endless. Icy pools once again hiding the passion that waited behind them.

"Vasilije."

She spoke his name like a plea.

"Invite me in, Sasa." As he spoke, he leaned in next to her, taking up the space between them.

The words almost caught in her throat, strangled by excitement and anticipation. She backed up across the threshold and beckoned him to follow her. "Come in, Vasilije."

His speed surprised her, and in seconds he had her by the throat, her back pressed painfully against the wall. His eyes hid no desire now. Now they were simply cold.

"Tatiana." He lifted his face in a sneer. "I can smell her here."

Fear raced through Sasa, and her heart slammed into her chest over and over as the name repeated in her head. He knew. He knew everything and he hadn't come out of love.

He'd come to kill her for what she'd done.

"Vasilije, please! I had no choice."

Rage flooded Sasa's senses as his anger leapt off him in spikes. Terror touched every part of her as she watched anger twist his face into a frightening expression of hate. His long fingers squeezed against the muscles of her neck and cut off the air from her lungs. Gasping, she thrashed against his grip, frantically grabbing at his arm.

"Don't do this! Please don't kill me. Please, Vasilije!"

"You killed Teagan and then lied this whole time, my sweet Sasa."

"No, please! Let me explain."

Sasa wrapped her hands against his muscular arm to push him away. The room began to swim before her eyes as he continued to tighten his grip around her neck.

The sadistic click of his fangs snapping into place echoed in her ears. The mouth that had brought her so much pleasure and tenderly taken what she'd so willingly offered now looked only deadly.

"Talk and maybe I'll spare your life."

Her throat tightened and she pleaded hoarsely, "I can't breathe. Please let me go."

Long seconds that felt like forever passed as he stared into her eyes while Sasa's head pounded to the rhythm of her racing heartbeat. As her eyelids drooped shut, he spread his fingers and she fell to the floor in a heap.

Sasa looked up at Vasilije staring down at her. She struggled to catch a few deep breaths and braced herself on the way to get up on her feet. His stare never left her, penetrating her, insisting she admit to her crime.

"Please listen to me," she begged as she stood to face him.

"I'm listening."

Sasa forced herself to meet his icy gaze and began. "My mother was sick. I told you I went to Quiterie for help. I couldn't stand to see her suffer any more. But I didn't have enough money. I couldn't let her stay in pain, so I told her about my gift. So in exchange for helping her, she performed spells for Mama."

"Helping her?"

"She reads cards, palms...I read people's emotions to

help her get a better read on them. Then Tatiana came in and Quiterie threatened to stop helping Mama if I didn't help Tatiana get revenge on someone. You."

Vasilije was quiet, and then asked, "By killing Teagan?"

"No! She said she wanted revenge on you and in return for making my mother a vampire, I had to help her. I swear I had no idea she was going to kill your friend. All I heard was your name and then she led me to Teagan's."

Sasa couldn't hold back the tears that had lain dormant since that night she'd watched Tatiana stake Teagan. As they poured out, she sobbed, "I'm so sorry, Vasilije. I had no idea. I didn't."

"And then you lied, pretending to be his girlfriend. Why? To get close to me?"

"She made me. She threatened to kill my mother if I didn't do as she said."

Vasilije stood silently staring down at her, his anger still coming from him in painful waves. Sasa reached out for him, afraid he'd push her away but needing to feel his closeness. As she touched his chest, he flinched, but he didn't recoil from her.

"I lied, but it wasn't a lie when we were together."

He turned his head and sneered, as if what she said sickened him.

"Please believe me. Everything else may have been a lie—being Teagan's girlfriend, knowing Tatiana, helping her—but when I was with you wasn't a lie."

Vasilije turned back to look at her and Sasa's heart sank. Everything in his face told her he didn't believe her.

"Not a lie? Why do you think that matters to me?

You're just another fuck. Nothing else. At least now I don't have to feel guilty about fucking Teagan's girlfriend."

"No..." Sasa touched his face, hoping to reach that part of him that had been so tender with her before. "Don't say that."

"You lie to me from the moment you meet me, and you want me to be nice? Nice to the person who helped stake one of my own?"

Every word that came from his mouth tore at her heart, his emotions almost overwhelming her. God, how she wished to hold him in her arms and make him remember their time together.

"I'm sorry. I didn't know. I had no choice. I couldn't let her hurt Mama. I never meant to hurt you. When I began to feel something for you, I did everything I could to help you. You have to believe me."

Vasilije ran his hand down her neck and let it rest softly on her collarbone. "I don't have to believe anything you say, Sasa. Why would I? Everything was a lie."

"No! What I did with you wasn't a lie!"

"No? So every time I was inside you, you weren't doing it to make me trust you?"

As he spoke, he pushed his knee between her legs and gently massaged her pussy through her clothes. His mouth caressed her neck as he whispered, "Not a lie, Sasa?"

Even as he taunted her, she couldn't help her body's reaction to him. He was so close, so desirable next to her. Every part of her yearned to grind against his thigh.

"Answer me, love."

Sasa ran her hands through his silky, black hair, pulling him to her. "Please don't do this."

His hands cupped her ass and squeezed as he pulled her to his stiff cock. "Don't do what, pet?"

"Don't use what I feel for you against me."

His teeth grazed the soft skin just under her earlobe and he whispered, "Like you did me?"

A chill ran through her body at his words. She had done that to him. But he'd meant more to her from the first moment his lips had touched hers than anyone before. Now he wanted her to pay for what she'd done.

Sasa shook her head and silently mouthed, "No."

"So I meant something to you, Sasa. And just what did I mean to you?"

How could she put it into words how much she cared for him as he stood glaring at her, his blue eyes icy slits in a face that seemed full of hate for her? Would he humiliate her if she told him how she felt?

"I care about you," she said quietly, choosing to safeguard her feelings against any possible attack.

"Mere words, love. Meaningless in your case."

"Then let me show you."

Tenderly, she pressed her lips to his and behind closed eyes, she hoped to feel even the tiniest bit of happiness begin to come from him. Instead, she felt only more anger. Rage exploded out of him, and he pressed her against the wall. "Not very convincing," he hissed.

"Please, Vasilije."

"Exactly what I had in mind."

His right hand shot out to grab her leg just above her knee, and he slid his palm roughly up to the hem of her cotton skirt. One painful squeeze of her thigh and then his thumb pressed against her sex, grazing her pussy.

"Wet? Isn't that a little pathetic, love?"

The pain of humiliation and rejection almost took her breath away. Without thinking, she scratched at him, catching her thumb on a fang. Slowly, blood bubbled up out of her skin and began to trail down toward her wrist as she watched his face, waiting for his reaction to her attack.

A growl came from deep inside him and reverberated against her chest. He brought her finger to his mouth as his eyes stared intently into hers. The anger seemed to be absent from them finally, replaced by desire. Never taking his gaze from hers, he slid her finger between his lips and gently sucked where his fang had nicked her.

Need coiled tightly inside her as Vasilije flicked the tip of his tongue over her finger. When he finally withdrew it from his mouth, her cunt ached for him.

"You taste so good, love."

He inhaled deeply and a sinister grin spread across his face. "What do you want, Sasa?"

She wanted him. All of him deep inside her bringing her to that delicious place she'd never felt before him. "Don't tease me, Vasilije. Tell me you forgive me and then give me what you know you want too."

His fangs made a quiet hissing sound as they slid back up into their home. "Forgive you? No. But I don't need to forgive you to fuck you. Call me open-minded."

Pushing him away, she straightened her clothes. "Yes, you do."

He lifted his head and closed his eyes, inhaling deeply once again. His eyes opened slowly and focused on her as he pressed close to her. "Your body tells me something else, love."

He was taunting her. He knew his effect on her and

was using it to humiliate her. Old hurts from men who never made her feel anything like he did resurfaced, and all she wanted to do was run away.

"Leave me alone! Get out of my house!"

Sasa fought against him, trying to get free, but he easily pinned her against the wall and smiled. "That only works in the movies and on TV, love. All I needed was your invitation to be able to come in any time I please."

Everything in her struggled between wanting him so desperately and wishing he'd stop tormenting her and leave her forever. The tug-of-war brought her emotions to just below the surface, but Sasa fought to capture some shred of control.

"Then just go because I mean nothing to you. Or if you're going to drain me, would you just turn me into a vampire so I can be with my mother?"

"I don't need another vampire to take care of, thanks."

Exhausted by her emotions, Sasa hung her head and worked to hold back the tears. "What do you want from me, Vasilije? Do you want to hear I want you? That whatever it is about you makes my body come alive at just the thought of you? That even now after everything you've done here that I'd forget everything to feel you inside me? Is that what you want to hear? Well, go fuck yourself. I didn't ask to get involved with you fucking vampires. Maybe if you hadn't been such an asshole to your ex-girlfriend, she wouldn't want to stake you or people you care about."

In a blur, Vasilije had her hands pinned above her head and was tearing her skirt and panties from her body. Before she knew it, his clothes had vanished, and his cock was pressed against her entrance. Seconds later, he thrust his body into hers.

God, she didn't want to want him like this. She didn't want to enjoy the sound of his groans so full of desire each time he rammed his cock into her. She didn't want to love the feel of his mouth, devouring her passion with a need that matched her own.

But she did. She wanted every inch of him, every moment of him, every touch of him.

Her body burned for everything he was.

"Let me touch you," she pleaded. She wanted to feel everything that was him.

As if her words were his command, he released his hold on her wrists and moved his hand to her lower back, pulling her even closer to him.

"Sasa..."

His deep groans filled her ears, and she caressed the dark strands that swung into his eyes with each thrust into her. Closing her eyes, she let her body enjoy him as she opened up to feel his emotions. Pleasure flowed through her, tinged with his continued rage at her. At Tatiana. At Jeremy.

His body invaded hers, joining them but taking what he wanted—selfishness that mixed with need so completely. Each thrust of his cock touched somewhere so delicious, so perfect she could almost forget the pain that slammed into her lower back each time she was forced into the wall, his strong fingers only adding to the effect as they were squeezed between her skin and the wall.

When he spoke again, Sasa heard the change in his voice and it almost took her breath away.

"I can't kill you, Sasa. I wanted to. I wanted to make you pay for Teagan...for what you've done. But I can't."

Vasilije stopped and Sasa opened her eyes, afraid of what she'd see. His blue eyes stared at her, not letting her look away as they searched for the answer to some unspoken question. Long black strands hung in his face, and as Sasa smoothed them back from his eyes, she felt his emotions war against one another. He wanted to hate her, but he couldn't.

There, with her back pressed against the wall and her legs wrapped around his waist, she waited for him to move or to speak, but he stood silently, his eyes fixed on hers. With her fingertips, she tenderly traced along his jaw line, the rough feel of stubble scraping against her skin.

Knowing the tug of war his emotions were creating inside him but needing some kindness from him, she closed her eyes and pressed her lips tentatively against his. Their softness betrayed his desire, but for a long moment he remained still and she feared he'd retreated inside himself, behind a wall of hatred she'd never get through.

Unsure if he'd simply deny her or worse, callously cast her aside, she slid her tongue along the seam of his lips, lightly touching his teeth. His hand on her lower back pressed against her sensitive skin, pulling her to him.

Sensing his desire was winning out over his rage, she ran her hand through his hair and pulled his head to hers as she intensified her kiss. He came alive under her lips' caress and slowly he matched her passion, his tongue gliding over hers as she felt his rage drift away.

His cock swelled inside her, pushing her body to accept him as he consumed her kisses like a man starved for love. He ground into her swollen clit and pulled her to him with his powerful hands as his need took on a life of its own.

The sweet beginning of her orgasm grew from inside her, and she tilted against him to take him deeper into her body. Vasilije read her cues and thrust faster, his face the picture of desire.

As the first wave of pleasure made its way to the surface, Sasa fisted his soft hair and moaned as she waited for the release only he could give her. "Vasilije...yes..." she cried as she waited in anticipation of that perfect sensation to arrive.

Suddenly, he lifted her off him and planting her on the floor, grinned a devilish smile at her. "No, I don't think so, love."

14

Sasa looked up at him, her expression a mix of need and confusion. Her body pressed against his, arching in search of that release that just seconds ago had been so close.

"Don't, Vasilije."

In a flash, he had her on her back on the nearby couch, underneath him as he hovered over her. Her brown eyes, wide with surprise, looked up at him as she waited for him to move. He watched as they became clouded with fear at the very real possibility of his anger returning.

"Don't what, love?"

His gaze slid down over her breasts, and he licked his lips before he bent down to take a rosy nipple into his mouth. It stiffened to an excited peak as he flicked the tip of his tongue over it. Sasa mewed her wish for him to continue, and he sucked the rouched nipple hard, eliciting a sound from her so filled with need that his cock surged against his belly.

Her hands grasped at his back to bring him closer and in a keening voice, she begged, "Don't make me wait. Please."

He loved to hear a woman beg for him to fuck her, but he wasn't ready to give in quite yet. Shaking his head, he crouched between her legs and slowly ran his fingertip through her wet pussy as Sasa pushed against his touch.

"Yes…yes," she said, almost sobbing.

His fangs snapped into place and as his eyes took in the sensual image of her glistening pink cunt, he ran his tongue over their sharp points. He'd get to what she wanted in a bit, but first he wanted something equally as delicious.

He slid his gaze to the vein that ran along the seam of her leg and traced the almost invisible pale blue line to her hip. Pressing his lips to her tender skin, he whispered, "Mine," and closed his eyes. He felt her tremble as he opened his mouth and then he sank his teeth into her.

His heartbeat pounded in his ears, nearly drowning out Sasa's soft cries as he drank eagerly from her. Her blood danced on his tongue as he sucked and lapped her vein. Each drop was more satisfying than the last, and he savored the taste of her as she once again nourished him.

When he'd drunk almost enough to harm her, he reluctantly flicked his tongue over her skin to close the holes. He remained at that most erotic spot on her body and pressed his lips to her skin. Sliding his finger through her wet seam, he plunged into her slickness. At the invasion, she moaned and he looked up to see her eyes closed and her face full of passion.

She felt tight around his fingers as he slid two into her and drew little circles with the pad of his thumb on her swollen clit. Her body told him she was edging closer to coming and he slid his fingers out of her just before her orgasm took her over, again denying her what she so desperately wanted.

Sasa opened her eyes and glared down at him. Her voice full of frustration, she asked, "Is this what you plan to do to punish me? Taking me so close and then leaving me there again and again?"

Smiling, he shook his head. What he wanted to do was ride her so hard that she begged to be free of him. Fuck her like he'd never fucked a woman before to punish her for what she'd done. Make her hate him so he wouldn't feel for her. And then leave her forever.

"Then what?"

Vasilije slid up her body and brushed his lips against hers, teasing her with the promise of what was to come. His tongue nipped at the corner of her mouth before he softly placed a kiss on that spot.

Cradling her face in his hands, he closed his eyes in ecstasy when she flicked her tongue gently against a fang, sending a jolt of arousal through his cock and balls. The effect she had on him....

"Vasilije, I need to know you believe me. That I had no choice."

Even as he lay there ready to bury himself inside her, he remained unsure he could ever believe her after all the lies. But he didn't care. Something about her touched him, something inside him needed her like he hadn't needed another woman in centuries.

"Don't. I don't want to think about that now."

The need to possess her raged through him and all remnants of anything sweet and kind were swept away, replaced by the solitary idea to make her his and his alone. He knew that was wrong. She'd already become too attached, and she was going to be hurt when he left. A second's worth of guilt flashed through him before he pushed it away.

He didn't want to think about that now either.

Vasilije pounded into her over and over, slamming against her body so forcefully she slid away from him with each thrust. Wanting something else, he leaned over and ordered, "On the floor, love."

Sasa followed his lead and lay back on the light blue carpet, her hair spread out around her and her sweet face angled up toward him.

"Other way, pet."

Vasilije flipped her over onto her stomach and pulled her hips toward his. Reaching around, he slid his middle finger through her wetness and massaged the engorged knot of nerves slowly. Bending over her, he let his cock slide between her cheeks and growled in her ear, "Consider this your punishment, love."

In one motion, he buried himself to the hilt in her wet cunt and began hammering into her like a man possessed. His ferocity surprised her, and she cried out at first, tiny squeals that should have made him stop but didn't. Over and over, he plunged into her, his hands holding her hips tightly as his fingers pressed into her flesh, marking her.

He waited for her to beg him to stop. He knew he was fucking her, plain and simple, like an animal. There was no kindness to his motions. On every thrust he expected her to plead for him to stop—at least to be gentle. But nothing.

All he needed was one word.

Very slowly, Sasa lowered her head, and he heard the tiniest sob escape her lips. Reaching out, he stroked her damp back and pulled out of her, still rock hard. Gently, he ran his fingertips over the red marks that were already beginning to transform to black and blue marks. His rage gone now, he kissed each bruise before he whispered in her ear, "Come, Sasa."

As she sat back on her heels, she looked up at him with a look of confusion in her eyes, as if she wasn't sure what awaited her. Silently, she took his hand as he pulled her to her feet and guided her back to the couch.

Vasilije pulled her down onto his lap and held her face in his hands to kiss her. He expected her to resist, but she kissed him like his mouth held the very key to her existence. Her tongue glided over his, making him want her. He moved to place his hands on her hips to raise her above him, but at the first touch of his fingers on her sensitive skin, she winced. Kissing her softly, he stroked her cheek, secretly guilty for hurting her.

"Ride me, Sasa. I need to feel you around me."

Slowly, she lowered herself onto him and he slid into her. She felt so wet around him. "God, I could drown in you, love."

As she found her rhythm, he squeezed her tender nipples and watched in awe as she fingered her engorged clit. Each swipe of her finger made her inner walls contract tighter around his cock. Selfishly, he pushed her hand away to replace it with his own, wanting to be the one who gave her what she'd waited so long for.

Big, brown eyes watched him, and she whimpered, "Vasilije, I need to come. Please don't stop."

He wouldn't have stopped for anything now, but her words touched him. He slid back the tender skin above her clitoris and circled the perfect bundle of nerves with his thumb. Sasa bucked wildly, riding him with abandon. He became focused on her orgasm, wanting to see her surrender to the sensual combination of his cock and fingertip stroking her to completion. Thrusting up off the cushion, he speared her deep inside.

Sasa hung on to his shoulders, squeezing tightly as her climax began its delicious voyage down her channel. Her cunt reflexively squeezed and released his cock, milking him as she came.

"Oh, God! Don't stop!"

Her release coated him in her juices, and she pushed down on him, seating him completely inside her. Exhausted, she collapsed on top of him and panted softly in his ear. She seemed so vulnerable at that moment, so small against him, that she could have asked anything of him, and he would have been powerless to deny her.

Quietly, she said next to his ear, "Am I forgiven?"

His fingers made long strokes down her back as he admitted to himself he couldn't stay angry at her. "Yes, love."

Sasa wrapped her arms around his neck and hugged him close to her body. "I love how you call me love and pet."

The feel of the soft, damp skin of her neck against his lips stirred his primal needs, and his fangs snapped into his mouth, ready to penetrate her. Sasa sat back to face him and without a word, turned her head and pulled her hair from her neck to expose her vein.

Vasilije took her chin between his fingers and turned

her back to face him. "I want to drink from you as I fuck you, filling you as I take from you."

Sasa moaned softly as she bit her lower lip.

"Tell me you want that, Sasa."

"You said once that there was no spell you used to make me want you. Did you tell the truth?"

Nodding, he smiled. "Yes. Whatever you feel is real."

Slowly, she began to ride him again, her hips undulating forward and back and creating the most incredible feeling in him. "I wish that wasn't true. Then at least I'd understand."

"Understand what?"

"Why it feels like you own my body—like I can't deny you. Even now I want to feel you deep inside me touching that spot and we just has sex a minute ago. "

"Let me give you what you want. Wrap your arms around my neck."

As Sasa held on, he stood up from the couch and carried her to the bedroom. Sliding her off him, he laid her down on the bed and wasted no time finding that spot inside her that brought her such pleasure. When he began to feel his body inch toward his own release, he nuzzled the tender skin under her ear where he'd take the gift she was to give him.

She smelled so good, so fresh, as he inhaled deeply next to her. "Sasa, you feel like I own your body because you're mine. You give me what I need."

Silently, she offered herself to him, and he sunk his fangs in, reveling in the familiar taste of her. As he gently drew her blood into his mouth, his cock exploded into her and her body spasmed around him, prolonging his pleasure.

When he'd finished taking from her, he lapped the holes with his tongue and lay there holding her. Her body was so warm next to his, so alive. So human.

Eyes closed, he let himself enjoy the feel of Sasa's fingers playing with the hair at his nape as the thought of staying like this forever settled into his mind.

"Vasilije, do you only take blood from me?"

He knew the answer she hoped for and wished he didn't have to say what he did. "No. I can't sustain myself on only your blood."

"Oh."

He didn't have to see her face to know she was disappointed. Her voice said it all. Vasilije lifted his head from her neck to look at her. "Sasa, I need the blood of my vampires, but I can't have that now. So I have to drink from humans."

"I understand." Her pouting mouth said she didn't.

"Do you?"

Sasa looked up at him, her dark eyes wide when she asked her next question. "Do you sleep with everyone you drink from?"

Shaking his head, he leaned in to kiss the tip of her nose. "No. Only you."

A twinge of guilt tugged at him. Why was he acting like her boyfriend? That's not what this was, even if the idea of staying with her did appeal to him.

Rolling off her, he lay back on the bed and stared at the ceiling, deep in thought about what he'd do to Tatiana when he finally got a hold of her. But Sasa wasn't done with her questions.

"Vasilije, what happens if you don't get enough blood?"

Turning toward her, he said, "I can't live without blood. It's not exactly like food for us, but we need it all the same. I'm an old vampire, so I can last a while, though, if I have to."

Sasa sat up. "But what about a new vampire? What happens to them?"

"They need the blood of their sire until they're ready to be on their own."

"Vasilije, I think my mother's getting sick. She only had a little blood at first and Tatiana isn't feeding her."

"Sasa, how long has your mother been a vampire?"

"Not even a month. Is that still new?"

"Very. How long did Tatiana feed her?"

"I think she gave her enough blood for three days."

"And she hasn't had any since?"

Sasa sadly shook her head. "Can you help her? You say she needs her sire's blood, but she can't get that and I'm not going to be enough, I guess. I know we're not...close...or family, but..."

Sasa's stammering told him she felt his emotions. He got up and made his way to the living room, dressing to leave. He may not be Sasa's mother's sire, but he could help her if it wasn't too late.

Standing in the doorway to Sasa's bedroom, he watched her as she dressed. Even now, after their time together, he wanted her still. But there were things to be done first.

"Sasa, after I help your mother, you will go to Tatiana."

"For my mother?"

"No. For me."

She made her way over to him as she slipped a t-shirt over her head. "For you? Why?"

He heard the jealousy that laced each word. "Because you're my spy now."

"Your spy? Maybe I don't feel like spying on your ex-girlfriend for you."

In a split second, he had her against him and his hand buried in her hair, not too rough but enough to let her know he was serious. "She was never my girlfriend. Well, not really. Now be a good girl before I have to punish you again."

"Not really? So why does she hate you?"

Vasilije bent down and gave Sasa a long kiss. "You're a very curious one, pet. Let's just say we crossed paths before."

"Is she your sire?"

The question was an innocent and valid one, but it struck a nerve anyway. Tatiana wasn't his sire, but she was responsible for the death of her. Her payback had been a long time coming, and it wouldn't be just stealing one of her boy toys this time.

This time she'd pay like she made Nina pay.

Vasilije turned toward the front door. "Didn't you ever hear the saying, 'Curiosity killed the cat', love?"

Sasa followed behind him, turning out the lights and locking the door. "And didn't you ever hear that satisfaction brought him right back?"

Just as the night he'd met her, Sasa marched by him and motioned for him to follow her. "It's a ways to Mama, so we'll take my car." She stopped and turned back to face him again with that quizzical expression she wore when she was ready to ask a question. Eyes squinted, she said, "Do vampires drive?"

Slipping the keys off her finger, he walked over to the driver's side door. "When we have a car we do. But I should warn you. I don't usually have to drive much, and I'm used to driving in London."

"This is Louisiana, Vasilije. You do know we drive on the other side of the road, don't you?"

"Not to worry, love. I learn quickly."

15

Sasa's mother was in worse shape than Vasilije had expected, but by four a.m., he had done everything he could for her. Leaving her in her daughter's caring hands, he found his way back to Teagan's place. It was the mess he'd left it after staking Jeremy, and the remnants of their struggle surrounded him as he headed toward the bedroom.

Teagan's sheets felt cool against his skin, and he stretched to let them touch every part of his body. Inhaling deeply, he took in Teagan's scent that still hung in the air.

Fucking Turkish cigarettes.

The memory of Teagan played on his mind, eating at his conscience. Tatiana had killed him out of revenge over some dumb kid barely out of his teens.

Fuck. And now I've staked Jeremy.

Vasilije covered his eyes with his forearm and told himself he wasn't exactly like Tatiana. But he was. He'd killed one of his own, no less. Now he'd kill her just the same.

Law or no law, the time had come for her to get what she deserved. How many years had passed since he'd promised to avenge Nina's death? Memories of a time long ago filled his mind as he drifted off to sleep.

The dampness from the river hung in the air, making the warm April night unseasonably moist. Crowds of Londoners strolled through the city, unaware of the danger that lurked amongst them, their fears of thieves and pickpockets upper-most in their thoughts as they made their way through the narrow streets of the English capital.

In the darkness, he waited to strike, his sire and her beloved sister beside him. He was a new vampire, just months into his new life, but he'd taken to it as if he were born to be such a creature.

"Vasilije, guide us to what we crave," Tatiana purred into his left ear as her hand pressed against the front of his breeches.

Just yards away from where they stood hidden in an alley way were two sets of lovers lost in each other's eyes, blind to what stalked them.

"No, Vasilije. There are many others to choose from. Spare them and let us move on."

Turning to Nina at his right, he saw her beautifully expressive face with eyes that pleaded for a reprieve for the couples. "Nina, you are a vampire. How can you entertain such silly romantic notions?"

"Precisely, sister. Vasilije has found us the perfect victims. Why do you bother with such nonsense?"

"I am his sire, Tatiana. If I command him to spare them, then spare them he will."

Vasilije waited for Nina's approval, sure the look in her eyes told him he'd get his way. But because of Tatiana's comments, he'd be forced to wait.

"Suit yourselves. I'll enjoy them for you."

"No!" Nina grasped for Tatiana, but she was already upon one of the males. His cries as she sank her teeth into his neck pierced the quiet street and his three companions fled in terror.

Nina pulled at Vasilije's sleeve. "We must go. If we don't, all three of us will pay for her carelessness."

He took hold of her and vanished from the alley and the bloodbath that Tatiana had created on the sidewalk in front of them. As he and Nina appeared just streets away, he heard the alarm go up in response to what was certainly Tatiana's murder of the man. People ran by them frantically to see the commotion as he and Nina hid in the darkness.

He shielded her with his body, forcing her to press against him. Blocking out the chaos that darted past them, he focused on the feel of her full breasts next to him. He slid his hand along her back down to her rounded ass and squeezed, enjoying the feel of her shapely globes even through layers of clothes.

"Not here, Vasilije," she said shaking her head.

"Yes, here."

Before she could protest again, his hands were burrowing under her skirts to touch her soft skin. He picked her up and held her hips as he pressed her against the side of the building, mere feet from the crowd of people still rushing to the spot they'd been just minutes earlier.

Kissing down her neck, he hovered over the very place he'd plunge his fangs into her and feed on the one soul he was meant to taste. He trailed his lips further down and planted kisses across the tops of her breasts as she quietly whimpered her approval.

Nina pulled his head up to meet hers and flashed her fangs at him. Just as he'd drink from her, she'd take his blood. Her lips pushed against his mouth, and quickly her passion rose to meet his as she swept her tongue into his mouth, grazing his fangs the way she knew would excite him.

"Vasilije, my love," she cooed into his ear as she delicately traced its outer edge with her soft lips.

Her voice thrilled him. Her words were like music to his ears. He loved when she gave herself to him, so open and tender.

Desperately wanting her, he freed his stiff cock from the breeches that strained against it. It sprung to attention, heavy and thick with need. In one swift movement, he lifted her skirts and pulled her to him, her soft skin pressing against the full length of him.

She looked beautiful in these moments before he buried himself in her, satisfying her need along with his own. Her dark eyes, wide with desire, stared into his, and he saw the vulnerability in them, a gentleness so foreign to many of their kind. Her mouth formed into a pout as desire coiled inside her and the words she'd speak to beg him to give her what she wanted formed on her lips.

Nina clung to him, wrapping her legs around his waist, as she impatiently rocked against him, drenching his cock with her moisture. "Give me what I want," she whispered as she kissed him again.

He positioned the swollen crown of his cock at her entrance and slowly pushed into her. Teasing her with just the tip, he only aroused her more, and she pulled at his hair, fisting it in her hands as she tilted her hips to take all of him.

Rearing back, he thrust forward and upward to bury his cock inside her scalding sheath as she cried out softly, "Yes! More!"

Repeatedly, he drove into her, making her moan his name as she tore at his clothes to touch him skin-on-skin. Her body gave him more happiness than he'd ever known, and the sounds of her pleasure flooded his ears, drowning out the noises of horrified Londoners just now finding Tatiana's carnage.

Close to exploding into the woman he loved, he slowed his pace to prolong the moment, but it was no use. As she sunk her sharp canines into his skin, his cock reacted, flooding her insides and triggering her release.

It was in these moments when she held him close, stroking his cheek tenderly as she took from him the very blood she needed to exist, that he adored her the most. He was the only vampire she'd ever sired, and since that day, he'd been devoted solely to her.

"Nina, love," he groaned as she slid her tongue lightly over the holes in his neck.

He watched in awe as she sweetly licked the last of his blood from her lips, smacking them like a child savoring the last of a sugary treat. Unlike any other vampire he'd ever met, Nina had retained the gentle innocence she'd possessed as a human. It shone in her eyes now when she looked up at him, smiling her happiness.

"Vasilije, my love, take us home so I can give you what you've just given me."

Her safety was his to ensure and nothing was more important to him. Kissing her softly, he held her to him and they vanished from their dark rendezvous, reappearing in their rooms below ground in a thirteenth century manor miles outside of London.

"Lie back on the bed. Let me give you what you need, love."

Vasilije closed his eyes as Nina lay on top of him, melding her body to his and positioning her neck near his mouth. "Take from me, Vasilije. Let me give you what no other can."

His lips trembled against her soft skin. No matter how many nights he'd fed from her, that spot just below her ear remained tender under his mouth. He stroked the area with his fingertips and trailed his lips softly over the skin, worshipping where he'd receive what he needed.

"Nina, love, thank you for all that you've given me," he said before piercing her vein to take the precious fluid she offered.

He'd tasted her countless times before, but each time just as the first drop teased his tongue he felt a thrill unlike anything else in the world. Tangy, coppery, she tasted like no one else he'd ever had. As his sire, she gave him the blood he required. Humans could provide him with blood, but not like Nina.

His sire.

As he savored her blood sliding down his throat, he remembered the night she'd made him the creature he was. The son of a sixteenth century prince and one of his concubines, he'd wanted for nothing growing up. Then upon his father's death, he and his mother were forced to flee west, penniless for the first time in his life. She'd died on the way, heartbroken at the loss of his father, and he'd somehow found his way to the lands of eastern France. Alone and hungry, he wandered aimlessly until Nina found him and took him in.

Since that night, he'd been hers. He'd grown accustomed to her sister's presence, knowing Nina believed herself to be responsible for her after the same vampire sired them both but *wishing it could be only the two of them, in love and together forever.*

Vasilije drew one last pull on her vein and flicked his tongue over her skin to close where he'd fed. Silently, he cradled her in his arms as she placed her head on his chest just above his heart, as she did when she was content.

"We need to find Tatiana, Vasilije. I need to know she's safe."

He stroked her soft hair that cascaded down her back, resenting once again how her sister intruded on their happiness. "You stay here. I don't want you out there if they're searching for us. I'll go."

Nina lifted her head and smiled slightly. "Who's the sire here?"

Rolling her onto the bed, he rose and made his way to the door. "You are, but that doesn't change what I said. I'll be back soon."

"Thank you, my love, for taking such good care of both of us."

Angry about being forced from Nina's arms, Vasilije focused his mind on a street near where Tatiana had attacked the man and in seconds was standing in the shadows as people moved past him on the nearby sidewalk. He listened for any sign she was close but heard nothing.

He'd had to do this more times than he preferred to remember. While Nina nourished his body and soul, her sister repeatedly threatened their very existence with her impetuous and selfish behavior.

"You came for me, Vasilije. I knew you would."

Vasilije turned and saw Tatiana at the end of the darkened alley. "It's not safe here. Come with me."

Instantly, she was in front of him, her hands roaming over his stomach toward the front of his breeches. "No, Tatiana. No."

She quickly worked to unfasten them and slid her hand in to stroke his cock. Her touch did nothing for him, but she wasn't deterred, instead falling to her knees to take him into her mouth. Vasilije yanked her up by her hair until she stood facing him, her expression full of hurt from his rejection.

"Don't. I've told you before I don't want you."

"Yes, you do. You haven't forgotten how it felt when we were together."

Tatiana moved to touch his face and he caught her arm, grabbing her by the wrist. "Your sister is the one I love. She can forgive that we were together once, so you can forget."

Wrenching her arm from his hold, she screamed, "No! You're meant for me, not Nina. I had you first!"

Before he could force her back home, she vanished, and Vasilije was left standing alone in the dark. Disgusted, he mumbled, "Serves her right if one of the hunters finds her and stakes her."

Resigned to his role, he walked into the light and began his search for her. He had no choice. If he had, he would have left her, but he knew Nina depended on him to keep her sister safe also. For hours he searched but to no avail. Just before dawn, he gave up to return home. Hopefully, she had returned already.

Their rooms were empty, and his body sensed dawn was just minutes away. He spotted Nina standing at the secluded area of a private garden far away from the house. Tatiana was with her, along with someone else he didn't recognize.

A man.

In horror, Vasilije watched as Tatiana struck Nina across the face, knocking her to the ground. The need to protect his sire—the one soul on Earth he loved—spiked in him, and he raced to help her.

He arrived in time to see the man next to her pull a stake from his coat and then everything seemed to move in slow motion. Nina squirmed on the ground in terror at the sight of the murderous weapon. The man's arm reared back and he lunged at her, trapping her underneath him. She fought his strength over her, fear in her beautiful kind eyes, as Tatiana stood by as the architect of her death never attempting to help her.

Vasilije charged the man, but it was too late. The stake plunged into her heart and his sire—the woman he loved— vanished into a heap of dust. He turned on her killer and took out his rage and pain with the only weapons he'd ever needed since that night when she'd made him a vampire, not caring if her killer became his killer too.

At the first signs of dawn, he left the remains of the man who'd taken the one creature on Earth that he truly cared for, and unable to return to the home he and Nina shared, fled to find shelter from the daylight that quickly approached.

A pang of loss cut at him as he struggled to push the memory of Nina from his mind. Even now, four hundred years later, the pain of betrayal he'd seen in her eyes just before she was taken from him tore at his heart. Now, at last, he'd get his revenge on Tatiana and finally honor Nina as he should have so many times over the last four centuries.

Vasilije lay there wishing he could forget everything from that time so long ago. Everything but Nina. The sound of the doorknob on the front door turning roused him from his bittersweet memories, and he waited for Sasa to come to him. Whatever she was to him, he needed to feel her in his arms, her body next to his.

Sasa said nothing as she entered the room and slid into the bed next to him. Her skin was warm as she placed her hand on his bare chest and slowly rubbed above his heart, her head snuggling into the space between his chin and shoulder.

"Thank you for helping my mother."

Vasilije said nothing but pressed a kiss onto the top of her head. He wasn't what anyone would call caring usually, but he couldn't let Tatiana's heartless disregard for her own kind hurt another innocent soul.

Sasa kissed him tenderly on his collarbone and whispered, "Tell me what's wrong."

"No."

"Is it something I can help with?"

"No."

It wasn't anything anyone could help with. Hundreds of years of guilt and regret that had become so much a part of him he wasn't sure he'd ever be free of them would only be helped by finally ridding himself of Tatiana.

Sasa wrapped her arms around him and laid her head on his chest. Squeezing him gently, she said, "Whatever it is, I can feel how sad you are."

"It will pass."

It always did. He'd felt Nina's loss for centuries and had become an expert at burying it under whichever vice was readily available. Power. Women. Sex. Gambling. Nothing ever took the pain away forever, but he'd learned to take whatever reprieve he could find.

For a long time they lay there silently in each other's

arms. He couldn't exactly figure out why, but just having Sasa near him made the old familiar ache that came from memories of the last time he saw Nina a little easier to bear.

She lifted her head off his chest and stared down at him for a long time before she spoke. When she did, her words surprised him.

"Vasilije, will you make me one of you?"

"No."

"Why?"

The sadness in her voice made him want to explain what centuries-old pain felt like. Instead, he said, "You wouldn't be a good vampire. You're too kind."

16

Sasa nervously ran her trembling fingers over the antique silver locket Vasilije held out to her. Oval and ornate, it sat safely nestled in his strong hand.

"Whose is this?" she asked as she took it between her thumb and forefinger and lifted it to eye level to examine it more closely.

"My sire's."

At the hollow sound of Vasilije's voice, Sasa looked up and saw something on his face that made her blood run cold. Never in her life had she seen such hatred in anyone's face. Not even Tatiana's.

"Why do I need to take this?"

Vasilije's eyes remained fixed on the locket in her hand. "She needs to believe I trust you...that you and I..."

Sasa waited for him to finish, but he turned away to grab her coat. "Remember who you're working for now."

As he slipped the coat onto her shoulders, Sasa felt his anger wash over her. Without thinking, she turned to him and threw her arms around him to hold him to her, hoping to ease some of his anguish. "I won't let you down, Vasilije."

Tentatively, at first, he returned the embrace, but then he ran the palm of his hand down the back of her hair. In a low voice, he said, "Be careful, Sasa."

She stood on her toes and planted a small kiss on his cheek. As she walked toward the door, the full reality of what she was about to do came over her. Turning to face him, she wondered out loud, "What do I do if something goes wrong?"

Vasilije came toward her and cradled her face in his hands. His expression changed from anger to something that seemed like sadness and a faraway look clouded his eyes. "Sasa, your blood is in me, just as I'm in you. If something goes wrong, I'll know. I won't let you be hurt."

His eyes, which had often either frightened or excited her, now comforted her with their hint of kindness. She had no idea what had happened between him and Tatiana, but she knew she owed it to him to bring her to justice for Teagan's death.

WHEN SASA ARRIVED at Quiterie's shop, only the dim light in the back of the store was lit. It seemed only proper that she'd meet Tatiana in the place she'd performed fraud so many times before. This time, though, she had to be more convincing than ever. Her life depended on it.

Carefully, she maneuvered through the dark voodoo store, dodging tables of handmade dolls and boxes of herbs as she headed for the office. Quiterie's favorite cinnamon incense drifted through the air and for a moment, Sasa was transported back to Christmastime at the house she'd shared with her mother and father as a young girl. Inhaling deeply, she let the memory come over her and mentally prepared for her meeting with Tatiana.

"Sasa, girl, don't dawdle. Come in," Quiterie called out.

As she stepped into the disheveled mess of the voodoo woman's office, Sasa's resolve faltered for just a moment at the sight of the vampire. Dressed in her usual all black, she was even more imposing than usual as she stood in four-inch heels that made her tower over Sasa and Quiterie.

"How is my little empath spy this evening?"

Each word seemed to hiss out of her as she stared down at Sasa. Standing as still as a statue near the door, she didn't see Tatiana's fangs. At least there was that.

"Fine, thank you." *Murderous bitch.*

"Sasa, how's your mama?" Quiterie asked, sounding almost sincere.

The answer she wanted to spit out was, "What do you care? You would've let her die if I hadn't helped you." That didn't seem wise, though, so she stuffed her resentment down and muttered, "Fine. She's fine."

"How nice. Now let's get to business. Quiterie tells me she had a visitor recently. Why would Vasilije be interested in speaking to our friend, Sasa?"

For a second, the news that Vasilije had found Quiterie and not killed her surprised Sasa and the urge to ask what he said nearly overwhelmed her. *Keep your wits about you, Sasa. You can't seem too interested.*

"He found out from some vampire in the Quarter who remembered seeing me here at the shop. I had to tell him I'm an empath to explain what I was doing here."

In a blur, Tatiana was standing in front of Sasa glaring down at her. "And just what else did you divulge to him?"

Craning her neck to look up at her, Sasa shook her head quickly as real fear raced through her. "Nothing. Nothing else."

Tatiana remained entirely too close for Sasa's comfort and turned her head to look back at Quiterie. "Does this work with what he asked you?"

"Yes. All he wanted to know was how Sasa used her ability to help me."

As Tatiana seemed to consider both their claims, Sasa wondered what else, if anything, he'd said to Quiterie. The very fact that he'd let her live told her he wasn't the vicious creature he tried to make her believe he was.

Tatiana turned back toward Sasa and sneered. With a long, manicured nail, she traced the line of her jaw, stopping under her chin. Lifting her face, she pressed the point of the nail into her skin.

"So how have you been succeeding in your task, dear Sasa?"

Fighting the need to stammer, Sasa worked to keep calm. "I think he's beginning to trust me."

She hoped Tatiana couldn't hear her heartbeat hammering in her chest. This was the most important part. She had to remember her role.

Dropping her hand, Tatiana raised one curious eyebrow. "Is he? And how did you accomplish that in the short time since we spoke?" Leaning in next to her, the vampire inhaled deeply. "I certainly hope you didn't make the mistake of sleeping with him."

"No, I did what I said I would."

"And what's that?"

"I listen to him."

A broad smile broke out on Tatiana's face, and she threw her head back as she let out a loud, full laugh. "You listen to him? And this seems to have worked?"

"Yes. I think he sees me as a friend."

Tatiana's gaze roamed from Sasa's eyes, down her body, and returned to study her face again. "How the mighty have fallen! There was a time Vasilije would have bedded you before he knew your name. Now he spends his time like a teenage girl talking about his feelings for hours. Well, I guess you're not really his type, so perhaps he hasn't become completely impotent as a vampire."

Sasa fought back the urge to explain exactly how much she was his type. And just what the hell did she know about anyone's type anyway? Like most men would choose her—a towering, bottle-blonde with teeth that could change them from a rooster to a hen in a split second of passion—over a woman who may not be supermodel material but at least had a kind heart?

"I wouldn't know about any impotence, Tatiana."

Spinning on her heels, the vampire flung herself into a chair near Quiterie's desk and crossed her legs. "You were very wise to heed my advice, Sasa. You have no idea how powerful his hold over you could be if you slept with him."

Quiterie spoke up. "Just like my mama always said. A man won't buy the cow if he can get the milk for free."

Sasa smiled, sure that this was nothing like what Tatiana meant. "I follow your lead, Tatiana."

"Very smart. So exactly why do you believe he's beginning to trust you?"

Knowing how she acted next was crucial to her success in helping him, Sasa drew out the moment and slowly put her hand in her coat pocket. Grasping his sire's locket, she withdrew her hand and held her palm out in front of her. The locket sat in the center of her hand, the light reflecting off it making it look almost magical.

"He gave me this. He said it's been in his family for ages."

Instantly, Sasa feared she may have slipped up with her reference to family. Did vampires consider their sires to be their family? As the thought of how she'd fix her blunder tore through her mind, she saw Tatiana's eyes open wide and stare at the locket.

"He gave you this?" Her voice was barely a whisper, and Sasa swore she heard it catch on the last word.

"Yeah. I think it was his mother's. You know how men are with stuff from their mamas."

Tatiana slowly rose from her chair and walked over to where Sasa stood holding out the locket. "It wasn't his mother's."

Before Sasa could slip it back into her coat, Tatiana had it in her hand and held it out in front of her. Staring at it, she said quietly, "Not his mother's."

Quiterie was up from behind the desk, and leaning around Tatiana, she looked up at Sasa. "It's very nice. Is there a picture in it?"

Curiosity surged in Sasa, and she reached to take the locket from Tatiana's hand. What had Vasilije's sire looked like? Would it even be her picture inside?

Tatiana released the locket, and it fell into Sasa's

hands. As the vampire stalked back to her seat, Sasa opened the locket but saw nothing. It was empty.

"It's still very nice, honey," Quiterie sympathized with a squeeze on her forearm.

"And you earned this just by being a shoulder to cry on? My, you are a clever empath."

The sharpness in Tatiana's tone brought back the reality of her situation, and Sasa quickly worked to change the subject. "So I believe in a few more days he'll trust me enough for what you plan to do to work."

The vampire's expression hardened along with her voice. "Plans have changed. I'll call you later to tell you what you're to do. Until then, don't leave his side."

Tatiana stood up and pushed past Quiterie to get out of the room. "And don't you go anywhere either."

"Tatiana, tonight..." She was gone before Sasa finished her sentence.

"Quiterie, I have to go. Take care of yourself. This lady is way more dangerous than you know."

Quiterie shook her head. "Baby, you be careful. You've got to deal with two of them, and you don't have to read fortunes to tell there's more to her revenge than meets the eye."

TEAGAN'S HOUSE was dark when she got back, and Sasa immediately feared Tatiana had already gotten her revenge. Unsure of what she'd find but hopeful it wouldn't be a pile of dust, she opened the front door and called out for Vasilije.

"It's Sasa. Are you here, Vasilije?"

Her calls were met with silence. Fear raced through

her at the thought that she was too late. She lurched forward, anxious for the sound of his voice or the sight of his piercing blue eyes, but in her haste she forgot the light and ran squarely into the couch, tumbling over it.

She landed on top of a body and felt the corded muscles of a man's neck under her fingers. "Vasilije?"

"I do like a woman who knows how to make an entrance. Even better is a beautiful one who throws herself at me."

Sasa sat up at the end of the couch and straightened herself in the dark. "Very funny. Why didn't you answer when I called for you?"

"I was lost in thought."

"Why are you sitting in the dark?" she asked as she turned on the lamp near the window.

In the light, she saw Vasilije lying back on the couch, dressed in jeans and a black t-shirt with his arms behind his head. "What happened with her?"

Sasa sat back down on the couch and began to tell him her news. "Vasilije, she got upset after I showed her the locket. She's planning on coming to you tonight."

She expected him to at least look interested in what she'd said, but he lay motionless, eyes closed. Had he understood?

"Vasilije, she wants you dead. She's planning on having me help her get to you. I'm supposed to stay near you until she calls my cell."

Opening his yes, a small smile crept onto his face. "Then I guess you better get over here, love."

"Typical male. I'm not kidding. Why aren't you more excited about this?"

"I'm excited. I'll be even more excited when you get over here."

Those blue eyes of his seemed to dance as he teased her, but Sasa wasn't amused. Grabbing the waist of his jeans, she tugged him to get him up on his feet, but he was stronger and pulled her down on top of him.

"That's better. Now what were you saying about me not being excited?" he teased as he ran his hands down her back and squeezed her ass playfully.

Sasa placed her hands on the couch next to his head and propped herself up. His face was so close and showed no evidence of concern over her news. "Vasilije, please listen to me. She's furious. Please don't underestimate her."

"You feel so good, pet."

He pushed his hips up off the couch, and Sasa felt his erection press into the area between her legs already feeling like it was on fire. Her mind told her body now was not the time to think of him snugly nestled inside her, but his body was more persuasive, and she gently ground her body next to his.

"I'm glad you're coming around to my way of thinking, love. And don't worry about her now. Just think about how good it feels when I make love to you."

Something in his voice sounded softer, almost sweet. And making love? He'd never called what they did together making love.

Sasa arched her back and pulled away from him. "What's going on with you? You never say making love."

Vasilije's hands pulled her to him, and he kissed her deeply, thrusting his tongue into her mouth to find hers. His passion surprised her and for a moment, she didn't respond. When he tugged at the back of her hair and moaned deeply, her resistance melted and her concern faded into the back of her mind.

His mouth feasted on hers as he removed her clothes. Sliding his hands over her back, he pulled her into his body. The feel of his strong hands rubbing her tender skin excited her, and she moved her legs to straddle him. Gently at first, she began rocking against him, sliding her excited nub over his hardened cock.

"That's my Sasa. Right there. Tell me what you want."

Leaning down, she continued to rock against him and whispered into his ear, "I want you to be careful."

"Not exactly what I was looking for, pet. But don't worry. I won't let her get me."

He glided his fingers over her back in long, languorous strokes that sent shivers up and down her spine. The idea that Tatiana would try to take him out of the world that very night and here he remained to be with her touched her heart but frightened her at the same time. God, he should be in her car miles away from there by now!

In her ear, he whispered, "Love, if you're concerned that this is my goodbye, don't be."

Sasa buried her face in his shoulder and closed her eyes tightly. The sound of the word goodbye made her chest hurt, but no matter how much she wanted to tell him she cared, the emotions she felt coming from him warned her not to.

Vasilije moved his hand from stroking her skin and his clothes seemed to vanish beneath her. Looking up at her, he took her face in his hands and cradled it sweetly. "Give yourself to me, Sasa."

His lips pressed against hers with an urgency that made her ache for him. She wanted so much to feel him inside her, touching her deeply as only he could, his body melding with hers.

Slowly he entered her and filled her body completely. Sasa's breath caught in her throat at the tenderness she felt from him, a tenderness he'd never fully expressed outwardly to her but existed all the same.

Later, as she lay next to him, she sensed that this time together had been a goodbye. Something had changed between them, something that she could sense as he held her in his arms. The idea of him gone from her life was almost as unbearable as Tatiana getting her revenge on him. In just a short time, he'd become so much more than any other man had ever been to her, and now he was going. She wanted to let him know that she understood, that she knew what they were and accepted that, no matter how much it hurt. But before she could tell him she understood why he had to leave, the quiet vibration of her cell phone hummed on the chair near them.

"Mama, what's wrong? Tell me. Do you need more blood?"

Sasa listened as her mother sobbed into the phone. Even in pain as she'd lain in bed for all those years, she'd never sounded this bad.

"Baby, I had Cam bring me home. I don't want to stay there anymore."

The streetcar crawled along St. Charles Street and Sasa prayed the next few stops before Canal Street would be empty. Her mama needed her, but at the rate the car was moving, it would take almost an hour to get home to her.

"Just hang on, Mama, and tell me what's wrong."

Her mother returned to sobbing again, and Sasa's anger grew by the second. Goddamned Tatiana! She'd promised she'd be okay after she became a vampire How'd she put it? "Healthy as a horse." Right.

"Is it blood, Mama? Do you need blood? I swear I

hope that Tatiana gets everything she deserves and more for what she's done to you."

A sound like a low moan came through the phone. "Don't say that, baby. Don't say that. She hasn't done anything."

Sasa's face grew hot in anger. Her mother was always too nice—too forgiving—for her own good. "How can you say that? She turned you..." Sasa looked around at the people near her on the streetcar and then continued in a low whisper.

"She was supposed to take care of you afterward, Mama. It wasn't enough to give you some supplies for just a few days. Vasilije told me as your sire she's supposed to make sure you're okay for much longer than a few days."

"No more of that. Just come home right now, Sasa. Please, baby."

"I'm coming. Just rest and wait for me."

After she hung up the phone, Sasa couldn't wait any more for the streetcar and jumped off, convinced she could run the last few blocks faster than the car filling with tourists and college students on their way to the Quarter.

Boarding the Canal Street car, she took her seat on the nearly empty streetcar and wished she'd asked Vasilije to come with her. Her mother was going to need his help again, and this time she might be even worse than last time.

His willingness to give his blood to help another sire's vampire made everything Tatiana had said about him so wrong. Her description of him as a vicious and selfish creature was so contrary to who he was when he was with Sasa.

Her feelings for him had grown out of those moments when he patiently drained enough blood from his wrist so her mother could have what she needed to survive. Still the old-fashioned woman she'd always been, she'd refused to put her lips on a strange man's skin, but he'd just smiled and offered to do it another, more appropriate way. But Sasa couldn't lie to herself. It wasn't just his kindness to her mother that made her care for him.

She knew he could be the man he'd claimed he was when they first met. His words had almost convinced her when he found out the lies she'd told about Tatiana and Teagan. But beyond the hurt at her betrayal was a closeness she knew he craved from her just as she did from him. His tenderness and acceptance of her once again was proof of that.

Sasa frowned in sadness as the thought of Tatiana exacting her revenge on him passed through her mind. In truth, she had no proof he didn't deserve her revenge. Maybe to her, he was everything she claimed him to be. She didn't care. Whatever he may have done or not done, Sasa couldn't let her kill him.

He meant too much to her.

That she likely didn't mean as much to him wasn't lost on her. No matter how tender he was when they were together, he'd never intimated she was anything more than someone he enjoyed. She'd never gotten the sense he was one woman's any more than she'd gotten the sense he considered her more than she was.

Sasa couldn't think about that now. It stung too much to think of him with another woman. Anyway, she had bigger, more immediate problems. As she had for so long, she once again needed to do whatever was in her power to take her mother's pain away.

The streetcar jolted to a stop at the end of the red line, and Sasa quickly ran the two city blocks to her house. All the lights were dark and from the street, it looked empty, but she hoped her mother had finally taken her advice and gone to bed. Opening the door, she fumbled for the switch on the wall, and in the light she saw Tatiana.

"Good evening, my little spy."

Her words dripped with sarcasm as she stood behind Sasa's mother, her hands around her throat. Sasa scanned her mother's face and saw no evidence of pain. Confused, she shook her head. "Mama, what's this all about? I thought you needed me."

"I'm sorry, baby. I didn't have..."

The regret on her mother's face told the story, but Tatiana continued, eager to explain how she'd duped her.

"No, she didn't have a choice. I'm her sire, and when I want her to do something, she must obey. It's just one of the benefits of being a sire."

The smirk on her perfect, pink lips signaled the woman's pleasure at her success, but Sasa couldn't let her think her win was complete.

"What about the responsibilities of a sire? You told me when you turned her she'd be healthy. Then you abandoned her, and another vampire had to feed her so she wouldn't die. If it weren't for Vasilije..."

The look of rage that flashed across Tatiana's face made Sasa step back in fear.

"Vasilije? He fed one of my vampires?"

Sasa watched in horror as Tatiana tightened her hold on her mother's throat. "Stop! You're hurting her!"

In a blur, Tatiana and her mother were inches away from her and the agony of Tatiana's hold was evident. Her mother looked so helpless hanging from her iron grip.

"Please, Tatiana. Please let her be. She's done nothing wrong. It's me you should be angry with, but I had no choice. She needed blood."

Tatiana seemed to consider Sasa's words for a minute and then discarded Sandra Lambert with a push toward the couch. She landed with a thud as her head bounced off the back of the furniture.

"Mama!"

Sasa moved to comfort her, but Tatiana stepped in between them. "Time for your confession, empath."

The urge to lash out raged through Sasa as she watched her mother reach out for her only to have her hand slapped away. "Sit still, you, and no more speaking. I want to hear her tell me about how having Vasilije naked under her is helping me get my revenge."

A chill ran through Sasa at the knowledge that Tatiana had seen her with him—proof she'd been lying. The twisted look of rage on the vampire's face told her she hadn't been wrong when she'd guessed Tatiana was far more dangerous than Vasilije.

"It wasn't what you think," she weakly mumbled.

Tatiana laughed and sat down in a chair, her long legs crossed in front of her. Even seated, she was the most powerful being in the room, and Sasa saw she knew it too. Twirling her long blond hair around her index finger, she looked up at Sasa.

"Do you want to know what I think?"

In truth, the idea of what this monster thought terrified her, but Sasa tried to put up a brave front, if for no reason other than her pride. After how she'd treated her mother, she deserved at least to know respect wasn't something she was automatically due anymore.

"Whatever you think, you're wrong."

"Oh am I, little girl? And just what reason other than fucking you would a man be naked under you?"

This was no use. There was no way she would ever believe her lies, and Sasa wasn't in the mood to think up any. "You're right. I slept with him, and there's nothing you can do about it."

Out of the corner of her eye, Sasa saw the look of fear settle into her mother's features. Turning toward her, she tried her best to calm her. "It's okay, Mama. He's not a bad man. Not like Tatiana said he was."

"Really, empath, I would think you'd be able to read others better. Perhaps it's a problem with vampires?"

"I read you just fine."

"Then maybe it's a good-looking man problem? I suspect someone like you doesn't find too many of them interested in spending time with you."

Each word felt like a slash into her skin, and Sasa winced at the pain. Foolishly, she snapped back, "You're just jealous because he wants me."

The evil smile that had accompanied her insults slid from Tatiana's face. "Wants you? He's had some of the finest beauties in Europe. Why would he now want some bayou bimbo? Trust me, empath. What he wants has never been anything like you."

Every insecurity Sasa had ever felt about her looks flooded over her and whatever bravery and pride she wanted to believe she had evaporated under Tatiana's withering stare. In seconds, she was merely Sasa, the empath.

"I don't care. I don't want to help you anymore. If you want revenge on Vasilije, you'll have to do it yourself."

Sasa waited for Tatiana's attack, but none came. She simply sat back in the chair and raised one eyebrow. When she spoke, her tone was wistful, as if she were remembering something from long ago. "I see he hasn't lost his skill in seduction. He always did know exactly how to get women to do anything he desired. It's the eyes, isn't it? I remember the first time he looked at me with those gorgeous eyes."

"Tatiana, please, let us go. Whatever your problem is with Vasilije, it has nothing to do with us."

"He can make a woman fall in love with him so easily. I warned you not to sleep with him, Sasa."

Sasa moved to take advantage of Tatiana's reminiscing and stepped toward her mother, who sat quietly obeying her sire. Gently, she stroked her hair as she had all those times she'd lain in bed, hoping to comfort her. Sadness over making her a vampire made tears come to her eyes. If only she hadn't done it, maybe things would have been different.

Sandra Lambert leaned into her daughter's touch and rested her head on her shoulder. Sasa decided to make one last plea. At least if she could get her mother to safety, she could deal with Tatiana on her own.

"Tatiana, please let my mother go, at least. She's done nothing to deserve your anger. Punish me, but let her go."

Finished with her memory, Tatiana turned to face Sasa, and she saw the same look she'd worn the night she'd met her. "Can you tell what I'm feeling now, Sasa?"

Sasa had intentionally blocked her emotions from the moment she'd seen her standing in her living room, but now she let her guard down and was stunned by the anger and hatred that surged toward her. Nearly over-whelmed by her emotions, Sasa closed her eyes, trying in vain to block them once again.

"I've waited so long, held in my vengeance for so many years and now when it's so close I can taste it, you want to take it away from me. He won't win this time. I won't let him."

"Tatiana, release her. Let her go back to my cousin's. She has nothing to do with your revenge."

An anguished look came over Tatiana's face. "He always did like the sweet and selfless type. Don't hurt them, Vasilije. Be gentle when you take them. Don't hurt Mama."

Tatiana's grasp on reality was quickly fading, if what she was saying was any indication. As she continued to ramble on about memories from her past, Sasa tugged at her mother to make her move.

"Mama, let's go."

Sandra Lambert sat as stiff as a board. "Don't bother. She won't move until I say so. And right now, you have some explaining to do. So tell me, Sasa, how much does he know?"

"Tatiana, I didn't have a choice. He found out some-how. I had to tell him, or he would've killed me. Please understand."

In a flash, the vampire was behind Sandra lifting her off the couch. "Wrong answer, empath. Now you'll be forced to understand how your betrayal affects those around you."

Before her eyes, Tatiana pulled a dagger out of her coat and dragged it across her mother's neck. In seconds, blood was pouring from the wound and the life was gone from her eyes.

"No! Mama!"

Tatiana dropped her onto the couch where she landed in a heap as blood drained from her neck. Sasa fell to her knees and sobbed as she cradled her mother in her arms.

Her betrayal had killed her mother.

"Mama, please forgive me. I'm so sorry."

Tears burned Sasa's eyes as the realization set in that she'd lost the most important person in her life. They streamed down over her cheeks, landing in the pool of blood on her mother's chest as she continued to sob uncontrollably.

"Time to go, empath. Don't make this mistake again, or next time it will be you who pays."

Sasa hugged her mother's body tightly to hers, refusing to release her. She didn't care if Tatiana killed her now. Nothing mattered anymore.

Tatiana yanked her hair, pulling her head back so she had no choice but to face her. The coldness in her voice matched her expressionless face. "Now."

"Kill me. Or don't. I don't care anymore. You've taken the only person I love away. Whatever you do to me doesn't matter."

"You're wrong, Sasa. I still have Vasilije to take away. And you're going to help me with that. So get up on your feet. It's time to go."

Sasa jerked her head forward and looked down into

her mother's lifeless eyes. "I can't leave her here like this. It's inhuman!"

"God, you're a stupid girl. No wonder he likes you. She's a vampire. Nothing human about it. But if this bothers you, let me finish it for you."

Stroking her mother's cheek, Sasa silently begged her mother's forgiveness for ever thinking turning her into a vampire was the way to end her suffering. Unable to endure the empty look in her eyes, she ran her hands over her eyelids to close them. Tatiana made a noise behind her and before Sasa could turn to see what she was doing, a stake grazed her arm on its way into her mother's chest. As she held her in her arms, the stake pierced her heart and she disintegrated into dust.

In shock, Sasa fell back onto the floor and stared at the remnants of what had been her mother. Blind with rage, she let the hatred in her heart take over and lunged at her mother's murderer.

"You fucking bitch! I hope he fucking stakes your ass!"

Tatiana caught Sasa just as she reached her and held her wrists in a vice-like grip. Sasa struggled against her, but it was no use. She was more powerful.

"Now, now, Sasa. Watch your tongue or I'll be forced to punish you."

"Go ahead. Kill me. I don't care."

Tatiana smiled and shook her head. "Not yet, love. You still have a job to do for me. Tonight you get to play bait, and he'll come."

"You're wrong. You said it yourself. He doesn't want me."

"He'll come."

Sasa pulled against her hold, but she wouldn't budge. "I won't help you get him."

Holding her wrists so hard she made tears come to Sasa's eyes, Tatiana glared down at her. "Yes, you will and one more word out of you and I'll do some damage to that pretty face he likes so much."

A second later they were racing toward where she planned to lure Vasilije to his death. When they stopped, Sasa opened her eyes and saw the sign above the cemetery in front of her.

Cypress Grove.

18

A half-hour after Sasa left, Vasilije was still on Teagan's couch, uneasy about the call Sasa had received from her mother. With every passing minute, his gut told him something was wrong. The timing was just too perfect. Two unanswered calls to her cell phone made him even more uneasy.

Afraid Tatiana might repeat what she'd done all those years ago, he headed for the only place he might get answers. Foregoing Sasa's preferred mode of transportation in favor of a method far more efficient, he focused on Quiterie's shop and in seconds was on the sidewalk looking at the storefront of the shop.

Unlike his first visit there, this time he saw a dim yellow light shining from the very back of the store. Trying the handle, he found nothing blocking him from a visit with the voodoo lady and entered the shop, ready for the possibility she actually possessed some magical abilities he hadn't seen in their first meeting.

Vasilije wove through the cluttered store, running his

fingers over mounds of polished stone and dusty containers of all things charmed as he silently made his way toward where the light came from.

"You're a long way from home, vampire."

Quiterie sat behind her desk and as Vasilije stepped into the office toward her, she motioned for him to come closer.

"Where's Sasa?"

"She's an interesting girl, isn't she?"

Leaning on the front of the desk, he focused on her black eyes, like two disks of coal in her dark face. "Listen, voodoo queen. You need to tell me where she is. Now."

"I don't know. Why you want to bother with her? She's not the kind of girl who can handle the likes of you."

"I don't have time to waste with you. Tell me where she might be."

"Did you try to call her?"

Vasilije had tolerated enough. She obviously needed some persuasion. His fangs slammed into his mouth with a terrifying click, and he grinned to let her see just what awaited her if she didn't begin to cooperate.

"One last time. Where is she?"

The sight and sound of his teeth did the job, and Quiterie's eyes grew wide in fear that gave him more than a tiny sense of satisfaction. "I don't know. She left right after Tatiana, and I haven't seen her since."

"When?"

"Hours ago. I haven't heard from either of them since."

Concentrating, Vasilije closed his eyes and attempted to pinpoint Sasa's whereabouts, but it was no use. She wasn't one of his vampires. The blood he'd taken from her wasn't enough. To sense her, she'd have to have taken his.

His mind racing at the thought of her with Tatiana, he opened his eyes to see Quiterie smirking, as if she knew what he was thinking.

"What you feel isn't real, vampire."

"What?"

"You care about her—or you think you do. But it's not real."

Crossing his arms over his chest, he studied this voodoo woman for a moment. Somehow, he bet, she was more show than anything else, more for tourists and desperate lovers than for anyone truly looking to experience magic.

"Sasa's not the only empath?"

Quiterie cackled, the sound coming from deep inside her belly, and threw her head back. Her white teeth flashed as she enjoyed herself at his expense.

Fed up with her, Vasilije turned to leave, not knowing where to find Sasa but sure his time was better spent than in Quiterie's presence.

"Magic is real, vampire, whether you believe in me or not."

As he moved to walk out of the office, he snapped, "Save it for the tourists."

"You need to show more respect. I am a mambo, a voodoo priestess. The loa serves me. What you feel for Sasa is what I made you feel. If I decide to reverse the spell, she's nothing to you."

Quiterie leaned back in her chair, making it creak under her weight, and said smugly, "And you're nothing to her."

Vasilije watched her fondle two black dolls in her lap. Was she serious? Had everything between him and Sasa been because of some fucking love spell?

"You better hope you haven't done anything that put her in danger because of this spell, or I promise you, I'll be back. And none of your voodoo nonsense will help you against me."

"Whatever happens to Sasa tonight will happen because of you. You've placed her in harm's way, vampire. Tatiana's vengeance is because of you."

Her words enflamed him, making his rage spike inside him, and instantly he was next to her with his hands around her fleshy throat. He slowly squeezed against the straining cords in her neck and pressed his thumbs against the front of her throat.

"I think you've hurt her enough, voodoo priestess," he hissed.

"And what have you done to her, vampire?" Quiterie croaked out.

The thought that he was to blame for what might be happening to Sasa made something snap in him, and in one swift movement his mouth was at Quiterie's neck ready to strike. His fangs pierced her skin and amid her cries, he gulped her blood down, relishing the agony he heard in her screams.

It didn't take long to drain her, and when he stepped away from her lifeless body, discarding it like a useless, empty shell, he wiped the blood that had spilled over his chin and jaw with the back of his hand. Not the revenge he sought, but not bad for an appetizer.

"Guess that's the end of you, Miss Quiterie. Now for the main course."

Heading toward Canal Street and away from the crowds in the Quarter, he ran through places Sasa might be. Just as he'd decided to try her cousin's outside the city, the cell phone in his coat pocket vibrated. The number on the screen was Sasa's.

"Sasa, where are you?"

His question was met with silence.

"Sasa? Answer me. Where are you? Tell me and I'll come there."

"My dear Vasilije. You sound positively undone by the idea of our little empath in danger."

The sound of Tatiana's voice taunting him stopped him dead in his tracks and her last words to him in London flashed through his mind.

Now I take something you cherish.

She wanted to hurt him again.

"I've already drained your voodoo lady, so don't think I won't kill you."

"Vasilije! Please don't try to find me. She's going to kill you!"

Sasa's voice so full of fear cut right through him. "Sasa, where are you? Tell me!"

Noises on the other end of the phone sounded like someone hitting someone and the sound of Sasa's cries told him Tatiana had already hurt her.

"When I find you, Tatiana, you're dust."

"Careful, love. I have your dear's life in my hands. If you want her, come to Cypress Grove Cemetery at the end of the Canal Street line. Follow the sound of her screams."

The line went dead, but it didn't matter. Nothing he could say would stop what had been set in motion centuries earlier. What mattered was that he got Sasa out of there before Tatiana did some real harm to her.

CYPRESS GROVE CEMETERY loomed in front of him, the name in wrought iron spanning two enormous white stone columns illuminated by the light of the full moon. The gate was padlocked, but to a vampire, this was no real impediment. Vasilije blocked out the sound of the street behind him and focused on trying to hear the sound of Sasa's voice. Gradually, he began to hear her soft whimpers.

Once inside, he walked slowly down the center aisle in this city of the dead lined with marble and stone crypts. A deep rust colored tomb caught his eye, and as he approached the fence that surrounded it, a cold brush of wind passed him. Suddenly, Tatiana appeared standing on top of the crypt, shielded by a sobbing Sasa.

"I told you he'd come, empath. He knows what I'd do to you if he didn't."

Sasa's desperate gaze met his, full of fear, and she cried out, "Vasilije, leave! She's never going to let me go, and I don't care anymore. She killed my mother."

Tatiana stifled her with a sharp squeeze. "Enough from you. He and I have unfinished business to discuss. Keep your mouth closed or you'll get what your mother got, and I don't think you want that, no matter what you say."

The need for vengeance coursed through him now as he listened to Tatiana refer to their unfinished business. For centuries, it had remained dormant, a dull ache he'd learned to live with and later ignore. The sight of her tormenting Sasa reminded him of those moments just before she let the hunter stake Nina, and that need for revenge was as acute as in the hours and days after Nina's murder when he roamed the Earth to satisfy his hunger for vengeance.

"Always one for the lambs, aren't you? She reminds me of Nina, love. Don't you agree?"

"Don't say that name. Get down here so I can send you to hell where you belong."

"Centuries later and you're still pining for my simpering little sister. Oh, that's right. She was also your sire. You've never properly thanked me for freeing you from her, Vasilije. Look at all you've been able to do without having to deal with her oppressive rule over you."

"You took away more than my sire."

As the last word left his mouth, Vasilije leapt toward the crypt, but Tatiana was faster and disappeared with Sasa before he reached them. Quickly, he scanned the rows of tombs around him but saw no sign of them.

"Can you honestly say you loved her, Vasilije? That weak thing?" Tatiana said loudly from somewhere in the row behind him.

"Yes," he answered, knowing what that one word would do to her. "Yes, I loved her for exactly that part of her, that gentleness you took advantage of."

Just as he guessed, hearing him profess his love for Nina enraged her and she appeared on a crypt in front of him, still holding Sasa to her. The effect of his words was written all over her face.

"Gentleness? What nonsense!" she barked, almost spitting out the words.

"That sweetness was something you never possessed. It's the reason I chose her when I could have had you."

"You're a fool! The weak, pathetic little birds could never make you happy. You know that. You need someone like you."

Vasilije shook his head in disgust. What he'd always suspected he now knew was true. Tatiana had killed Nina because of him. "I never loved you. It was always her."

He was treading on dangerous ground. At any moment, she could snap and hurt Sasa, but centuries of hate for his sire's death made him continue. "You think you're like me? No. You're cruel. Nothing more."

Tatiana walked to the end of the cement tomb and dangled Sasa by the neck, choking her slowly. "Cruel? You think ridding the Earth of weaklings like this is cruel? I'm doing them a favor. Take this one, for example. Even to you it must be obvious that she's in love with you. And what has she gotten for that? Her mother's dead and you've been spending our time talking about how much you love a ghost."

The pain on Sasa's face as Tatiana spoke stabbed at him. His need for revenge couldn't trump her safety, so he'd do what he must to save her. Anything to make sure Tatiana didn't do to her what she'd done to Nina because of him.

"Let her go. She's done nothing and she means nothing to me."

"So you don't care if I kill her?"

Vasilije couldn't bear the sadness in Sasa's eyes from his words. Focusing on Tatiana, he shook his head. "You want me, not her. She's nothing. I'm the one who chose Nina over you. I'm the one who took Alex from you."

Abruptly, Tatiana jerked Sasa back onto the top of the tomb and released her hold on her neck. Gasping for air, Sasa fell to her hands and knees.

"You're right. You're the one I want." Pulling Sasa back to her feet, she added, "But my feminine intuition tells me you do care for our little empath friend here, so she'll stay with me."

In a blur, they disappeared from in front of him, and Vasilije jumped to the ground and listened for Sasa. In the distance he heard her scream, "The tree!" and he turned to see the two of them near a sprawling old tree about a hundred yards away.

"Let her go, Tatiana," he yelled as he walked toward them. "Let her go. You want me."

Face-to-face with Tatiana, he saw she held something in her hand. As the moonlight glinted off it, Vasilije recognized it as his dagger he'd lost just before Nina was killed.

"Remember this? Remember how when Nina wasn't around we'd slit their throats and feed like gluttons?"

He remembered. He remembered how Nina had scolded him for being so heartless, forbidding him from doing it again. Even now, her gentle words admonishing him echoed in his ears.

"We were monsters when we didn't have to be. You should have listened to Nina."

"And become like her? No, thank you. And I'll have you know, this dagger has done its job many times since that night I took it from you, including earlier tonight."

Vasilije knew what was next. In a painfully ironic twist, she planned on killing someone he cared for with the dagger he'd so callously used for the same purpose so many times before.

He couldn't wait any longer. Ready to avenge Nina's death and Sasa's torment, he lunged at them, catching Tatiana off guard. Both women fell to the ground, and Vasilije felt Sasa roll away from them. Happy she was safe, he took off after Tatiana when she fled. He caught up with her on the steps to a crypt that resembled the church his father had been buried near. Standing in front of an archway to a central tomb flanked by columns below a domed roof with a cross, Tatiana waited for him —for a showdown that was four hundred years in the making.

"I got rid of Nina but still you didn't want me. I loved you. I would have killed for you."

Vasilije stared into her troubled eyes. "You did. You took her away from me. Now I'll do what I should have done that night instead of mourning her."

Wrapping his fingers around the sharpened wooden stake concealed in his coat pocket, he squeezed the weapon tightly. Tatiana would be the second of his kind he'd kill. He'd be just like her now.

It didn't matter.

Without a word more, he slipped the stake out and cocked his arm back to finally send her from the Earth and avenge his sire. She saw what he planned to do, but it was too late. Before she could react, he'd done what he'd wished he could have that night centuries ago.

The stake pierced Tatiana's chest, and he plunged it deep into her heart. Then she was gone and all that was left was dust floating in what seemed like slow motion to the marble steps in front of him. Emotion threatened to overtake him as he watched the particles fall into small piles on the pristine white marble. He couldn't truly regret his actions, no matter what their laws dictated, but what he'd done turned his stomach all the same.

Vasilije closed his eyes and hoped somewhere Nina heard his thoughts. *I'm sorry, Nina. For not saving you then and for what I had to do now.*

The breeze rustled the leaves on the tree behind him, and he turned to see Sasa lying on the ground. His dagger stood proudly erect from her chest, a symbol of Tatiana's hate for him. Staggering toward her, he fell to his knees beside her. Still alive, she looked up at him, the sadness in her eyes from his words earlier replaced with pain and fear.

"Sasa."

Her voice barely a whisper, she said, "I'm glad I got to say goodbye, Vasilije. But I need to know. Is she gone? Please tell me I can die knowing my mama's murderer is gone."

Nodding, he stared down at the dagger and the deep red stain that surrounded where it met her body. "She's gone, pet."

A small smile formed on her lips, and she closed her eyes. "Thank you."

She was fading away right before his eyes. Each breath caused her chest to rise a little less until at last she was silent. Vasilije's whole body ached at the reality of Sasa out of his world. Whatever they'd been to one another, she deserved better than what she'd gotten.

19

Vasilije had to work fast if he intended on turning her. He leaned down to press his lips to her neck and heard her take a shallow breath. If she could hang on just a few seconds more...

"Sasa, stay with me. Don't go."

Her eyelids fluttered slightly at his words, and Vasilije's heart leapt at the promise of enough time. As he had with her before, he held her in his arms and sunk his fangs into her neck, tapping her vein. The blood flowed slowly this time, and he was forced to pull at the vein harder than usual. Sasa whimpered softly at the pain but never moved.

When he'd taken enough and Sasa's life hung by a thread, he pulled away from her and watched her begin to change. The beautiful skin with its deep glow paled before him, leaving only the warmth in her eyes that gazed up at him softly.

"Vasilije?"

"Almost, love," he said as he brought his wrist to his

mouth. One sharp push into his own skin and his vein opened. Gently, he pressed it to her lips and held her head as she began to drink from the one who would forever be her sire.

The feelings she ignited in him as he watched her drink his blood were exquisite. Never before when he'd sired a vampire had he felt so alive. So happy. His skin danced with pleasure, and with each gentle pull of her mouth, the experience almost overwhelmed him with sensations. Closing his eyes, he accepted all it offered.

When she'd drunk all she needed, she touched him softly on the hand. "Take me home."

He lifted her in his arms and cradled her next to his body as she rested her head on his shoulder. In seconds, they were back in the Garden District at Teagan's house.

Home.

Vasilije gently laid her in the bed and took his place next to her. More beautiful than he'd ever seen her, she looked up at him with concern in her eyes.

"I thought you didn't want another vampire to take care of."

He stroked her brown hair that seemed even darker now against her pale skin. "Always with the questions. That mouth is going to get you in trouble, love."

"What's going to happen to me now? I'm all alone now that Mama's gone."

Sasa closed her eyes and squeezed them tightly. One tear escaped and rolled down her cheek. He'd lived alone so long it never entered his mind that being alone would upset her. But she wouldn't be alone.

She'd be with him.

Vasilije bent down and softly kissed her lips. Cradling

her in his arms, he whispered, "You're not alone. You're mine and you'll be with me."

"I never got the feeling you wanted anyone with you."

Smiling, he winked and said, "I didn't. Now rest."

For once, Sasa didn't argue with him or question why. Closing her eyes, she quietly drifted off to sleep next to him.

"Vasilije, I'm hungry."

Sasa's need woke him, and Vasilije stretched the sleep from his muscles. Instinct told him it was still daytime, but a new vampire's need for blood didn't follow a schedule. Opening his eyes, he saw her staring down at him, or more precisely, his neck. Her brand-new fangs were ready for their first use, and her dark eyes were wide with hunger. Vasilije placed his hand on the back of her head and guided her to his waiting vein.

"Come, Sasa. Drink."

Her lips softly pressed against his skin and for a moment, she kissed him. Warm puffs of air drifted over his skin and then tentatively, she opened her mouth. The first touch of her fangs thrilled him, and his cock filled from desire of what would follow her feeding.

Sasa sank her teeth into him eagerly, and she opened his vein instantly, as if it were second nature to her. Any hesitation she felt vanished as his blood flowed into her. Vasilije held her tightly to him, loving the erotic sensation her mouth pulling his vein created in him.

Each draw sent a jolt through him straight to his cock, which stiffened more by the minute. The feeling wasn't exclusive to him as Sasa began to run her hand over his chest and stomach, her moans vibrating against his skin as she drank.

She slid her hand down to his hip and around the base of his cock. Slowly, she matched the rhythm of her mouth with her hand, stroking him as she took the precious fluid she needed and only he could give.

Vasilije fisted her hair and tugged gently. She was driving him mad with desire, but he knew she needed more blood. Her first real feeding, it was too important to rush, but God, he wanted to. How badly he yearned to be inside her, her body surrounding him like it was meant to be only his.

"Vasilije." Sasa leaned back away from him and licked her lips.

With the tip of his finger, he caught a drop of blood that sat just beneath her lower lip. Sliding his finger into her mouth, he ran it across her tongue and then one of her fangs. The effect was immediate.

Sasa closed her eyes and moaned her pleasure. "Don't tease."

Up and down one fang and then the next, his finger followed the action of her hand on him. Aroused, she sucked his finger into her mouth and glided her tongue over it seductively, opening her eyes to watch the effect of her teasing on him. Then she stopped, let go of his finger, and smiled.

"What is it you're always saying about my mouth getting me in trouble? Is this what you mean?"

Unwilling to wait any longer, he nodded and pulled her on top of him. She was wet and her pussy slid up and down his cock until he was slick. The feeling made the tip of his cock feel like it was going to explode if he didn't bury himself in her now.

Sasa wanted to play more, but that could wait. Grabbing her hips, he positioned her over him and speared into her as deeply as possible. For a moment, he held her still, her body pressed to his so closely they appeared as one being. She made a pleading noise for him to continue and moved her hands to his chest to brace herself when he finally moved again.

Like an animal, he plunged into her wet cunt over and over as she bucked up and down on him, meeting his every thrust with one of her own. This was the true joining of a sire and his vampire. Wild. Uninhibited. She was his—a mate made for him. He was also hers, meant to take care of her every need.

Sasa rolled her hips forward and back, taking him deeply into her. But he wanted more. Pulling her down onto his chest, he growled next to her ear, "Give yourself to me, Sasa."

Pushing aside her hair, she exposed her neck as she continued to ride him. His body roared with desire when she whispered breathlessly, "Take me. Take me now. I want to feel you drinking from me as you fuck me."

Teeth that had pierced thousands of veins strained to bury themselves in her neck. Pulling her to him, he found the spot just below her ear and sank his fangs into her. The first taste of her blood and its familiar and exciting tanginess sent a rush through his body, and he pumped wildly into her, unable and unwilling to control his need to feel that release that came only with another of his kind.

He greedily took every ounce she gave, forcing

himself to remember his appetite was more than she as a new vampire could handle. Her blood aroused him, energized him, and sustained him like no other had in centuries, and it took every bit of self-control he possessed to keep his desires in check.

Her moaning and talking didn't help his restraint. New to her life as a vampire, she was experiencing her body's reaction to sex in a far more heightened way, and the more timid Sasa from her human life was no more.

Reluctantly, he slid his tongue over the holes in her skin to close them. Rolling her over, he hovered over her body before he plunged into her again, his desire no less powerful than before, but his appetite satisfied, at least for now.

EVERY INCH of her body felt more alive than ever before. Her lips tingled as he kissed her and slid his tongue into her mouth to play with her fangs again. Now she understood how excited she'd made him when she'd done that to him.

Each time he plunged into her, his cock caressed nerve endings never before touched. Wrapping her legs around him, she longed to have him as close to her as possible. Her skin buzzed with excitement each time it came in contact with his.

Sasa opened her eyes to see him staring down at her, his blue eyes betraying none of the passion his body and words expressed. His fangs flashed white against his blood stained lips, and she would've been frightened if she weren't his.

His vampire.

His emotions were easier to sense now that he'd sired her. A feeling of happiness flowed from him to her, mixing with desire and making each sensation he created in her more intense.

"I want more."

"More what, love?"

Running her hands over his smooth, muscular back, she whispered, "More. More blood. More you. More this."

"Take from me, Sasa. I'm your sire, the only one in the world who has what you most need."

His words excited her with the thought that he was hers. Her sire. But what was she to him?

Any thoughts of that slipped away as his cock grazed that sensitive spot deep inside her and sent her orgasm tumbling through her. Clinging to him, she scratched and clawed his back as she came like she never had before. Vasilije pumped into her sweetly, dragging her release out until he held her to him as his flooded her insides.

After a few moments, she wondered out loud, "Will it always be like that?" and prayed his answer would be yes.

"If not better. There are benefits to being with one of your own."

Vasilije rolled off her and pulled her close to him so her head rested on his chest. Silently, he played with her hair as she listened to the slow rhythm of his heartbeat. Even more than when they'd been together before she was turned, she felt safe in his arms.

And curious to know what her new life held in store for her.

"Tell me what I need to know about who we are, Vasilije. I want to know everything."

"Same old Sasa. I think I'm even getting used to you."

Sasa lifted her head and met his gaze. "Good. You won't be so irritated by my curiosity then."

Vasilije raised one eyebrow and grinned. "Never irritated, love."

Sitting up, she folded her legs under her and leaned toward him. "Good. Now what do I need to know?"

He put his arms behind his head and a thoughtful look came over his face. "Anything you need you can get from me. Blood. Security. Everything."

He never said anything about love. Was that implied in everything? Or did he have someone for love? "How many of me are there?"

A cute smirk formed on his lips. "There's no one else like you, Sasa. Not in four hundred years have I met another Sasa."

"I meant how many other vampires have you sired."

"Hundreds."

His casual answer did nothing to help her fears that she was just one of many. "Where are they?"

"Everywhere. If I want them, all I have to do is call them back to me."

"Oh. So none stay with you?"

Just saying the words made her feel lonely, and the sadness of losing her mother flooded back into her heart.

"I have one now in addition to you, but he'll soon be free to leave."

"Will I have to leave?"

As she waited for his answer, anger ignited inside her. She hadn't chosen to become one of his vampires, and if he'd sired her only to send her out into the world alone, she'd be better off left for dead in that cemetery.

"I don't send them away as much as let them go when they ask. You may find you want to leave."

"And wander through the world alone and lonely?"

He smiled up at her as he caught a lock of her hair between two fingers. "As long as I live, you'll never truly be alone again, Sasa. Staying or leaving will be your choice."

His answer gave her no more sense of any love for her than his feelings did, but something in it satisfied her. Laying her head back on his chest, she thought about how lonely he must have been since losing his sire. Quietly, she said, "I'm sorry about your sire."

Vasilije said nothing and kissed the top of her head. Opening herself up to his emotions, she sensed the sadness he felt over Nina's death. Part of her was jealous, but she understood his sadness. Now that he was her sire, she felt an undeniable attachment to him. More than just a lover, he was the one who'd given her life—this life. He was her creator and her protector. The mere idea of an existence without him made her sad.

But now wasn't the time for those thoughts. A new world awaited her, and she would have him by her side to experience it all.

NEW TO HER LIFE, Sasa enjoyed the world Vasilije had given her. By day, she rested in his arms protected from the world outside their bed. By night, he gave her everything she craved—his body and his blood—and taught her how to live as a vampire. For the first time in so long, she knew security. Then one night, news came that ripped these feelings of safety from her.

Vasilije held her close, but she sensed something was wrong. He avoided her gaze, but she couldn't let him worry about whatever it was alone. For everything he'd given her, she wanted to be more than just his vampire. She wanted to show him she could be his partner in everything, good and bad.

"What's wrong?"

He remained silent for a long time and then said the words that took her breath away. "I have to leave, Sasa."

"No! Why?" A thousand reasons for his leaving raced through her mind, each one more painful than the last.

"The Archon wants me tried for staking Tatiana and Jeremy. If I stay, he'll make sure I'm punished."

"But you were protecting me from Jeremy almost raping me and avenging Nina's death with Tatiana. You were justified in what you did."

Vasilije frowned and shook his head. "No, love. Perhaps I can claim justification for Tatiana's staking, but I killed one of my own vampires for a human when I staked Jeremy. In our world, that's forbidden."

Sasa clutched his arm tightly. "Then we'll leave New Orleans. Wherever you go, I'll go. There's nothing keeping me here if you're not here."

"No. I need to go into hiding. You'll stay here with LeClerc. I've arranged it with him. You'll be safe there."

"So you've figured it all out? You'll just leave me here while you go off. It's that easy for you? How am I to survive? You're my sire."

"Sasa, it's been two months. You don't need the blood of your sire to survive now. LeClerc can take care of that. And you know everything you need to know to survive."

His methodical way of explaining everything away

made her want to explode. He was leaving and it didn't seem to matter much to him at all. It was all decided, and she was just expected to obey.

But she didn't want to obey.

Sasa backed away from Vasilije and struggled to control her emotions. Everything she had was being ripped from her. "No! Please don't do this. Don't leave me with strangers. Let me come with you. You just said I know everything I need to know to survive. I can handle myself no matter where we have to go. It's you I'll miss, not the blood or the lessons on how to be what I am."

"You'll be safe here. I have to know you'll be safe. I can't explain now, but this is something I have to do alone."

"Then keep me safe! Don't do this!"

He felt like an empty void when Sasa opened herself up to feel what this was doing to him. She had to convince him to change his mind.

"I don't want to be alone. You promised me when you made me a vampire I would never be alone again."

Vasilije said nothing as he looked away. Sasa couldn't hold back the tears anymore, and they streamed over her cheeks and down her jaw. He was going without her. Something deep inside her warned she might never see him again.

Vasilije wrapped his arms around her and held her close to him. Everything she sensed from him now told her he wasn't sure they'd see each other again either, but he pressed his cheek to the top of her head and said, "I promise you won't be alone. Trust me."

By the end of that night, she was without him at LeClerc and Yvette's, alone in a house full of her own kind but essentially strangers to her. Each day she waited for some word from him, but none came. Weeks grew into months, and LeClerc successfully convinced the Archon that Vasilije had been justified in Tatiana's staking. After numerous meetings with Sasa, he had even commuted his sentence in Jeremy's case because of Vasilije's long history as a sire. Word had been sent to his London home, but still he never returned.

Finally, one night as she walked the French Quarter, the connection she'd felt since their first night together as vampire and sire—the connection that had been her lifeline to him since he'd left—disappeared. She couldn't sense his presence anywhere in the world. She was now just as he'd been for centuries.

Truly alone in the world without a sire.

20

The sun set below the nearby mountain range, leaving a sky of deep purples and oranges. Vasilije gazed out at the natural beauty left behind by the day. Centuries since the last time he'd enjoyed the feel of the sunlight on his skin, the last remnants of each day still fascinated him here. He remembered as a child playing in the sun among the guards assigned to watch him, the only son of the local prince. Surrounded by sisters from his father's wife and numerous concubines, he'd lived a life of special privilege then.

Those days were long behind him now, but his return to the land of his Romanian home had been the refuge needed to secure his safety after his escape from New Orleans. It had also renewed him, preparing him for the duty he'd finally perform for his kind. For the duty the Sons of Navarus would fulfill.

His time in seclusion hadn't been entirely because of his actions in New Orleans. The real truth the Louisiana Archon's actions came to light in those days right after he'd arrived in this place. Tatiana's attempt on his life hadn't been merely because of her desire for revenge. She was part of a much larger plan by the Archons against the Sons of Navarus. From this point on, he'd be a marked man, wanted dead by the vampires intent on ruling their world as they saw fit.

But he wouldn't be alone. There were others like him in the Sons of Navarus, and together, they would fight against the Archons. And there was Sasa.

As darkness enveloped the countryside, Vasilije waited for Sasa's arrival. He'd called her to him minutes earlier and knew as one of his vampires, she'd have no choice but to obey his command.

Whether she wanted to or not.

The place she was to come to was as different from her home in New Orleans as night was to day. Nestled in the Carpathian Mountains, the land surrounding the town of Suceava was quiet and secluded but close enough to modern necessities. It wasn't the French Quarter, but she'd get used to it.

It would be an adjustment, but in time, he hoped she'd come to love the area as he did. Her addition to his life here would be the last piece to make it complete. He'd missed her in their months apart. Closing his eyes, he replayed the last night they'd spent together, enjoying the memory of her taking what she needed from him as they joined together once again as sire and vampire.

"Vasilije?"

He opened his eyes and there she stood, mere feet away from him. Every cell in his body craved her touch as his heart called out to her.

"Sasa, come."

She looked at his outstretched hand and stood motionless, her face the picture of hurt. Looking up at him, she leveled her gaze on him. "And this is what you expect? You leave me alone for months, not knowing if you were dead or alive, and then the moment you call, I'm expected to drop everything and come to you? I'm not the woman you left all those months ago, Vasilije."

Not exactly the reunion he'd hoped for.

As she spoke, his gaze wandered over her body. He'd missed the feel of her against him. She may have been standing in front of him in jeans and a sweater, with enough attitude to put off the average man, but he imagined her naked and far more amenable to his ideas.

"Are you even listening to me?"

"Yes."

"Yes what? Yes, this is what you expect from me, or yes, you're listening to me?"

He couldn't help but smile. The effect she had on him was unlike that of any other soul in the world. If any other of his vampires spoke to him like that, he'd punish them severely, and God help any human who dared to do anything like that. But Sasa was different.

"Yes to both. Now come here and stop fighting me."

She walked toward him reluctantly, as if she were resisting her very nature, but she didn't have a choice. She was his. Gradually, her eyes softened and the woman he'd left all those months ago stood in front of him.

"Sasa, I missed you. If I've ever hurt you, it was not what I wanted."

Without speaking a word, she told him she'd missed him too. Wrapping her arms around him, she pressed her body to his and looked up at him with that gentle expression that always made him want to possess and protect her. Her mouth—the mouth that had given him such exquisite pleasure, lied to him, and even driven him to the brink of madness once or twice—waited for the touch of his, begging to be kissed.

"I haven't forgiven you for not coming back to me. And where is this?"

Dipping his head down to kiss her, he slid his tongue along the seam of her lips. "Romania. And you will. Give it a minute, love."

Feigning annoyance, she turned to walk away, but he pulled her roughly to him, pressing her back against him. Cupping her breasts under her sweater, he squeezed her excited nipples as she pushed against him. Moaning, she gave a quick wave of her hand and her clothes disappeared, leaving her naked next to him.

"Nice trick, pet."

"I've been practicing."

Her words struck him like a hand across the face, and the thought of her with another man sent a possessive rage coursing through his body. She was his. His vampire. His woman.

Spinning her around, he lifted her, and she wrapped her legs around his waist. She hung on to his neck while she fumbled with his pants' button as he carried her to the bedroom. Pushing her back onto the bed, he shed his clothes with a smile.

"Get on your hands and knees, love."

In front of him, Sasa's body waited for his touch. With his hands on her hips, he climbed onto the bed and eased her back toward him. Arching her back, she opened herself up to him, wanting him as much as he wanted her. Slowly, he slid into her and stilled, reveling in the pure pleasure she gave him.

He'd missed this. The feel of her body surrounding his like a glove, so snug even as she dripped with arousal. The memory of their last time together like this flashed before him, and he ran his palm over her soft skin to her neck and back again, worshipping the feel of her beneath him. That time had been full of rage. This was about love.

Moving in and out of her, he found a sweet rhythm. He was in no hurry. If this was the way he spent the rest of his nights, he could leave this Earth knowing happiness once again. But he needed to see her, to see those dark eyes so full of desire staring into his.

He reluctantly left the warmth of her body and turned her to face him. Hovering over her, he was struck by her beauty. From the moment he'd first touched her, she'd enchanted him. Now as his vampire, she threatened to undo him. Looking up at him, her knowing eyes still tinged with innocence, she seductively ran her tongue across the tips of her fangs.

"Don't tease me, Vasilije. It's cruel, and you shouldn't be cruel to me."

Cruel.

Her words touched his heart, and he lowered himself to her, knowing she had no understanding of how she affected him. Every night without her had hurt, like a piece of him had been ripped away leaving an open wound. Now she was with him again, and mere words from her endangered any control he thought he'd possessed.

She clung to him as they made love, as if she feared

losing him once more. Never. He wouldn't let that happen again.

He slid his teeth over her skin and next to the tender spot just below her ear. "Give yourself to me, iubita."

She did willingly and as the first of her blood entered him, she tightened around his cock and cried out in ecstasy, surrendering her arousal to him even though he knew she'd been hurt by his absence. As his own release surged into her, he felt at home. Truly, after so long, he was home.

In the silence between them as they lay together in one another's arms, Sasa kissed him and asked, "What was that word you used? Iubita?"

"It's a Romanian word."

"What does it mean?"

Stroking her cheek, he looked into her eyes so filled with curiosity and love and kissed her.

"Beloved."

EPILOGUE

Vasilije watched as the men filed into the room and positioned themselves backs against the wall. Each was a member of the Sons of Navarus like him—charged with protecting those most ancient of their race, the Order of Macaria—and powerful in their world. They'd come in response to the Order's call for them to take a stand against the corrupt Archons who threatened their world.

They stood silently, watching for who would speak first, who would say the words that would seal their fate. Vasilije stood from his chair and motioned to Sasa to close the door.

"I'm glad you all made it. How many years has it been since the vampire world needed the Sons? What vampires have feared for eons has finally occurred. The prophecy has come true. The Archons have begun their plan to eliminate the Order to secure their own power. Each of you is in danger as you stand here because to do away with them, they must first get rid of us. They want to eliminate us from our world so the Order is defenseless. But not all of you have agreed to this. Some of you have had this handed down from your sires. Know that none of us will judge anyone who chooses to leave now."

"Fuck that. If you're a coward, you deserve to be judged."

Vasilije turned to the youngest of the Sons, a vampire with an all-American boy look and the body of an athlete. "Dante, relax. Not everyone is up for a fight like you."

A few murmured their opinions quietly, and Vasilije raised his hand to silence the group. "If anyone wants to leave, there's the door. Know that we wish you the best. But I'm not going to let those fucking Archons wipe out what vampires have had throughout history. I won't let them kill the ancients. I promised to give my life for the Order. The Archons have already tried to kill me, and they'll try again. Obviously, Dante is with me. Who else is?"

The six other men stood looking straight ahead as they considered the most important decision of their lives. One stepped forward, and Vasilije braced himself for what would come next.

"I need to know this isn't a you-as-the-leader thing. If that's what this is, I'm out. I'll take out as many Archons as I can and take care of myself."

Vasilije grinned with relief. Declan's comments weren't surprising. Teagan's brother, he was bigger and more menacing than Vasilije's friend had ever been. Dark and secretive, he hadn't liked him since the day he turned Teagan, and the feeling was mutual. But he was a Son of Navarus above all else.

"No, I'm no more powerful than any of you. The

Archons want us gone because we're protectors of our race. We're also what they aren't. Sires. That gives us great power, and most of us have taken advantage of that power to sire many vampires who are loyal to us. This isn't about me, Saint. This is about keeping those sterile fucks from getting any more power than they already have. If we don't, we can all kiss our world goodbye."

"Fine. Then I'm in," Declan mumbled as he stepped back toward the wall and folded his arms across his chest.

Vasilije waited for more questions, but none came. "Well, then I guess introductions are in order. Some of you may not know all of us. That's Saint."

"I'm guessing by your attitude that your nickname is ironic?" Sion asked.

Declan grimaced and Dante chimed in with, "No. He's called Saint because he doesn't fuck his vampires. We'd call him Virgin, but then he'd have to stop fucking humans."

Declan moved to grab Dante, but Vasilije stepped in between them. "Relax, gentlemen. Sion, why don't you tell us who you are? Some of us might not know you. It's been a long time since the Sons were all together."

Sion stepped forward and stuffed his hands in his pockets. Lean, he was the picture of logic and reason, rarely giving a sign of his emotions. "I'm Sion, I inherited this job when my sire was staked in the 1940s, and if you need to know how something works, come to me."

"Glad to have you here, Sion. We know each other from way back, and I think you'll all find him to be a valuable member of the group," Vasilije added.

Dante leaned in and whispered next to his ear, "Interesting group so far, Vasilije. A sexual deviant and a geek."

Vasilije ignored Dante's comment and continued. "Terek, I think almost everyone here knows you."

A dark-haired man with piercing green eyes bowed slightly and smiled. "I get around."

"Still all about the mystical stuff, Terek? I bet that gets the ladies to give in quick," Dante joked. "Maybe that's what you need, Saint. A little Terek mojo to fix up your problem."

"One more fucking word out of you and we'll be seven, not eight," Declan growled.

"And Ramiel and Thane. Gentlemen, good to have you here. If anyone knows about the prophecy, it's these two," Vasilije said as they nodded silently. "What they know has been handed down from ancient times. Their sires were two of the original Sons of Navarus. Gradually, over the centuries, all the other vampires believed to carry the true knowledge of the prophecy have been lost and only Ramiel, Thane, and two other vampires remain."

The other Sons regarded the two men, who stood silently staring back at the group. Ramiel was the biggest of all the men assembled and had the face of an angel, but eyes as black as night. Thane only slightly smaller, but his eyes showed a kindness absent in the other vampire's.

Vasilije continued, "You may be the most important of us here. If we intend on stopping the Archons, we'll have to figure out where the secret of the prophecy is hidden."

Turning to the last member of the group, Vasilije moved to shake his hand and smiled. "And last, but not least, Nico. Haven't seen you in a long time. I wasn't sure you'd be in for this. This wasn't your responsibility, and considering your sire, no one would blame you for bowing out."

Every bit as Greek as his name, Nico was dark with olive skin and black hair. The most ancient of the Sons of Navarus, he'd been turned in ancient Greece as a young man and appeared as if one right out of a Greek myth. "Not in on giving those Archons what they deserve? I just need to know we'll be taking some of them out. This won't be any fun if we're staying all law abiding."

Vasilije nodded. "That may be what we have to do. Right now, we need to find out what their next move is and go from there. I've already spoken to someone who will act as our spy with them. I know I'm still a target, so that's something that's going to be a reality from now on. But we need to know who's next. So we've got to protect the Order and protect ourselves."

"Like a vampire A-Team?" Dante joked.

"Jesus Christ, let it be me they want to kill next so I don't have to listen to this asshole anymore," Declan grumbled.

Vasilije shook his head. "Not exactly, Dante. The Archons want us dead because of who we are, but even more so, they want the Order of Macaria liquidated. That's far more than just the people in this room. And we're not exactly do-gooders here. We'll get dirty if it calls for it."

"Then where do we go from here?" Sion asked.

"As soon as my spy tells me what she knows, we'll know what to do. Until then, make yourselves comfortable. Old monasteries have a lot to offer."

IT WAS STILL hours before sunrise, but Vasilije and Sasa lay in bed relaxing from a long night with the other Sons of Navarus. Sasa rested her head on Vasilije's shoulder as she listened to him explain what the group was planning, and when he finished, she asked, "Do we know who the Archons have chosen now? Whose vampires are going to have to live in fear like I do?"

He kissed the top of her head and tipped her face up to look at him. "You have nothing to fear, love. No matter who they send, I'll do what I have to."

"Why are they doing this?"

"Archons by ancient law can't sire vampires. This was supposed to ensure impartiality, but all it's done is ensure that the ruling class is corrupt. They only have to obey the magistrates, and they're usually their sires. It's a rather incestuous system. They want to be sires, but even more, they want power. It's not enough for them to be the law and order of our world. They want what the ancients have. They're sick of being the cops of the vampire world."

Sasa sat up and crossed her legs under her. "So why not just go around the Archons and tell the magistrates what they're doing? The magistrates wouldn't allow them to harm the most ancient and revered members of our world."

Vasilije sighed and rested his palm on her knee. "Because as their sires, they're unlikely to believe us over their vampires if we don't have proof. All we have now are a few dead vampires and Tatiana's attempt on my life."

A look of fear came across Sasa's face at the mention of what they went through in New Orleans. "Can the group beat the Archons? Are the Sons of Navarus strong enough?"

"The Sons of Navarus are as ancient as the Order. Long ago, when our world began with Hades' daughter Macaria, the Sons was created in dedication to the human she loved—the first vampire. Since then, whether recruited or given the duty by their sire, there have always been eight vampires charged with protecting the most important of all vampires, the Order of Macaria. For many years, the Sons were forgotten, and peace reigned in the vampire world. But the prophecy was always there, always a reminder that if the Archons attempted to eliminate the Order, the Sons would be needed."

Sasa wrinkled her nose. "I love you, Vasilije, but you don't appear to be someone I'd think would be a protector of vampires, other than your own, of course."

"I've been part of the Sons of Navarus since the late 1800s. I was asked because of the number of vampires I've sired. Sires like me, with many vampires, are very useful to the Order."

"So how can we ever hope to beat the Archons?"

Running his hand up her thigh, he paused at the seam of her leg next to her hip and smiled. "We're strong, and there's safety in numbers, love. Between all of us here, there are almost five thousand vampires we've sired. Each one of us comes with a lot of loyalty. I don't think the Archons have thought about that."

"Will that be enough?" Sasa asked unmoved by his hand slipping under her panties.

"Our vampires alone? No. But together, we can use their help to protect the Order and get what we need to show the magistrates what's going on. And if we can unlock the secret of the prophecy, we'll be able to stop the Archons, no matter what their sires believe."

As much as he knew Sasa was concerned about what was happening in their world, Vasilije didn't want to talk anymore. There were other things he preferred to do before he had to meet with the group again, and they had nothing to do with Archons, magistrates, or anyone other than Sasa. He tugged at her nightshirt to bring her to him, and she landed gently on top of him. Kissing her softly, he savored the feel of her lips against his. Whatever the world outside their bedroom held in store for them, he didn't care at that moment. All that mattered was how much he wanted to make up for lost time.

He ran his hands through her hair, reveling in the softness against his fingers, as she moaned her desire against his lips. Cradling her face, he held her in front of him and spoke what his heart had hidden since he'd made her one of his own.

"Sasa, you mean more to me than anything in this world. Every day without you was torture but know that I had no choice. I need you to know that no matter what happens with the Archons, you're everything to me."

Closing her eyes, Sasa smiled and kissed him tenderly. "I forgive you. But I need to know you won't do that again. I want to be a part of this. I know I'm not one of the Sons of Navarus, but I want to stop these bastards as much as you. Let me help you do that."

Vasilije began to speak, but just then his cell phone began vibrating on the dresser across the room.

Placing a kiss sweetly on the tip of her nose, he whispered, "Don't move. We'll pick this up right where we left off."

Vasilije answered and the voice on the other end of the phone spoke one word and then there was silence. Turning to Sasa, a knot formed in his stomach as he repeated what his spy had reported. They'd chosen the next one of them to die.

"Saint."

ABOUT THE AUTHOR

K.M. Scott writes contemporary romance stories of sexy, intense, and unforgettable love. A New York Times and USA Today bestselling author, she's been in love with romance since reading her first romance novel in junior high (she was a very curious girl!). Under her Gabrielle Bisset name, she writes paranormal and historical romance. She lives in Pennsylvania with a herd of animals and when she's not writing can be found reading or feeding her TV addiction.

Be sure to visit K.M.'s Facebook page at **https://www.facebook.com/kmscottauthor** for all the latest on her books, along with giveaways and other goodies! And to hear all the news on K.M. Scott books first, sign up for her newsletter today and be sure to visit her website at **http://www.kmscottbooks.com**

BOOKS BY K.M. SCOTT

Complete Club X Series Box Set

NeXt SERIES

Notorious (NeXt #1)

Infamous (NeXt #2)

Ravenous (NeXt #3)

Ambitious (NeXt #4)

Flirtatious (NeXt #5)

Mysterious (NeXt #6)

Sensuous (NeXt #7)

Desirous (NeXt #8)

CORRUPTED LOVE TRILOGY

If I Dream (Corrupted Love #1)

If You Fight (Corrupted Love #2)

If We Fall (Corrupted Love #3)

Corrupted Love Trilogy Box Set

ADDICTED TO YOU SERIES

Crave (Addicted To You #1)

Adore (Addicted To You #2)

Shatter (Addicted To You #3)

Claim (Addicted To You #4)

Addicted To You Series Box Set

PROJECT ARTEMIS SERIES

In The Darkness (Project Artemis #1)

K.M.'S BOOKS ARE IN AUDIOBOOK TOO!

BOOKS BY K.M. SCOTT WRITING AS GABRIELLE BISSET

SONS OF NAVARUS SERIES

Vampire Dreams Revamped (A Sons of Navarus Prequel)

Blood Avenged (Sons of Navarus #1)

Blood Betrayed (Sons of Navarus #2)

Longing (A Sons of Navarus Short Story)

Blood Spirit (Sons of Navarus #3)

The Deepest Cut (A Sons of Navarus Short Story)

Blood Prophecy (Sons of Navarus #4)

Blood Craving (Sons of Navarus #5)

Blood Eclipse (Sons of Navarus #6)

Blood Ascendant (Sons of Navarus #7)

The Sons of Navarus Box Set #1

The Sons of Navarus Box Set #2

DESTINED ONES DUET

Stolen Destiny (Destined Ones Duet #1)

Destiny Redeemed (Destined Ones Duet #2)

VICTORIAN EROTIC ROMANCES

Love's Master

Masquerade

The Victorian Erotic Romance Trilogy